From *Come and Go*

He came back with a tray of decanters and glasses and one glass filled with claret. Hawkes wondered why, possibly some medicinal requirement which was no concern of his. The red wine was set in the middle of the table and Wilkins began pouring sherry while Charles idly snapped his fingers as a man does when he is trying to remember something.

Hawkes turned aside to take a cigarette from a box and light it; as he turned back to the table he saw something which, for a passing second, he took to be a wisp of smoke from an ashtray. But it was not; it was too big, it was too transparent, it had a definite shape, it rounded and solidified by rapid degrees, it was a small brown monkey in a little red jacket and cap. What was so particularly shocking was that no one except himself seemed to find anything odd about it. The taller Latimer stretched out a long finger to rub the creature behind the ear and it tilted its head like a cat. Wilkins moved the wineglass towards it with a smile and said: "There you are. Is that all right?"

Hawkes, who had been holding his breath, gasped and gasped again as though he had fallen into a tank of ice water. It seemed that he could not get his breath. James Latimer turned suddenly with an expression of concern.

"My dear Mr. Hawkes! Are you ill—what is it?"

Hawkes, quite beyond speech, pointed a shaking finger at the monkey, who took off its little cap and made him a polite bow.

Charles came round the table with long strides and threw one arm round Hawkes' shoulders. "It is only Ulysses; what upsets you so? That is my monkey; did Richard not tell you?"

"But," gasped Hawkes, "but he is a ghost."

Books by Manning Coles

Ghost Books
Brief Candles, 1954
Happy Returns (English title: *A Family Matter*), 1955
The Far Traveller (non-series),1956
Come and Go, 1958

The Tommy Hambledon Spy Novels
Drink to Yesterday, 1940
A Toast to Tomorrow (English title: *Pray Silence*), 1940
They Tell No Tales, 1941
Without Lawful Authority, 1943
Green Hazard, 1945
The Fifth Man, 1946
Let the Tiger Die, 1947
With Intent to Deceive (English title: *A Brother for Hugh*), 1947
Among Those Absent, 1948
Diamonds to Amsterdam, 1949
Not Negotiable, 1949
Dangerous by Nature, 1950
Now or Never, 1951
Alias Uncle Hugo (Reprint: *Operation Manhunt*), 1952
Night Train to Paris, 1952
A Knife for the Juggler (Reprint: *The Vengeance Man*), 1953
All that Glitters (English title: *Not for Export*;
Reprint: *The Mystery of the Stolen Plans*), 1954
The Man in the Green Hat, 1955
Basle Express, 1956
Birdwatcher's Quarry (English title: *The Three Beans*), 1956
Death of an Ambassador, 1957
No Entry, 1958
Concrete Crime (English title: *Crime in Concrete*), 1960
Search for a Sultan, 1961
The House at Pluck's Gutter, 1963

Non-Series
This Fortress, 1942
Duty Free, 1959

Short Stories
Nothing to Declare, 1960

Young Adult
Great Caesar's Ghost (English title: *The Emperor's Bracelet*), 1943

Come and Go

a ghostly comedy by
Manning Coles

The Rue Morgue Press
Boulder, Colorado

Contents

To
A.J.C.H.

. . .busy here and there. . .
I KINGS XX:40

Cast

Richard Scroby
Miss Angela Scroby, his aunt
Wilkins, his manservant
Hawkes, a journalist
Millicent Biggleswade

Toni le Chat
Pépi the Crocodile, Philippe Morand
Jules the Cosh
Fingers Dupré
} Crooks

James Latimer
Charles Latimer, his cousin
Ulysses, a monkey

Police, postmasters, innkeepers, etc.

Scene: Paris
Time: 1958

About Manning Coles

MANNING COLES was the pseudonym of two Hampshire neighbors who collaborated on a long series of entertaining spy novels featuring Thomas Elphinstone Hambledon, a modern-language instructor turned British secret agent. Most of Hambledon's exploits were aimed against the Germans and took place from World War I through the Cold War, although his best adventures occurred during World War II, especially when Tommy found himself, for one reason or another, working undercover in Berlin.

Some of those exploits were based on the real-life experiences of the male half of the writing team, Cyril Henry Coles (1899-1965), who lied about his age and enlisted under an assumed name in a Hampshire regiment during World War I while still a teenager. He eventually became the youngest officer in British intelligence, often working behind German lines. After the war, Coles first apprenticed at John I. Thorncroft shipbuilders of Southhampton and then emigrated to Australia where he worked on the railway, as a garage manager, and as a columnist for a Melbourne newspaper before returning to England in 1928.

The following year his future collaborator, Adelaide Frances Oke Manning (1891-1959), rented a flat from Coles' father in East Meon, Hampshire, and the two became neighbors and friends. Educated at the High School for Girls in Turnbridge Wells, Kent, Manning, who was eight years Coles' senior, worked in a munitions factory and later at the War Office during World War I. In 1939 she published a solo novel, *Half-Valdez*, that failed to sell. Shortly after this disappointing introduction to the literary world, Coles and Manning hit upon an idea for a spy novel while having tea and began a collaboration that would last until Manning died in 1958. Coles continued the Hambledon series for an additional three books before he died in 1965.

Critic Anthony Boucher aptly described the Hambledon books as being filled with "good-humored implausibility." That same good humor—and a good deal more implausibility—is to be found in the collaborators' four ghost books, which began with *Brief Candles* in 1954 and included two other books featuring the ghostly Latimers, *Happy Returns* in 1955 (published in England as *A Family Matter*) and *Come and Go* in 1958. A fourth ghost book, *The Far Traveller*, which features a displaced, displeased and deceased German nobleman who finds a movie company employing people of the most common sort invading his castle, appeared in 1956. Appearing in the U.S. under the Coles byline, they were published in England under yet another pseudonym, Francis Gaite. Boucher described this new venture "as felicitously foolish as a collaboration of (P.G.) Wodehouse and Thorne Smith."

For more information on the authors see Tom & Enid's Schantz' introduction to The Rue Morgue Press edition of *Brief Candles*.

CHAPTER I
Gentlemen of the Press

RICHARD SCROBY paid off his taxi and walked into the entrance hall of the block of flats where he lived. He nodded to the porter and then wished he had not because the movement almost made him lose his balance. He strode on quickly towards the lift at the back of the hall and took himself up, although his flat was only upon the first floor looking over a service road and a row of lockup garages at the back. The porter said: "Good night, sir," and looked after him for a moment with faint amusement.

Scroby opened the gate of the automatic lift to prevent himself from being carried away if anyone else should summon it and leaned his head against a nice cool pane of plate glass. He did not feel at all well and he was also in a state of nervous irritation very unusual with him. He had been to a dinner of the Old Boys' Association of his old school; the amount he had drunk had gone to his head and made him muzzy and uncertain of his balance. He pulled himself together, stepped out of the lift, and turned into the passage leading to his own flat.

Not a very interesting set of fellows there at this dinner; of course, each year it was a matter of luck who would attend. It was extremely pleasant to meet Hawkes again, Hawkes who had been in his form and was now a journalist. He had left London to work in Paris and Scroby had mislaid his address; it was satisfactory to have it again.

Braced by the pleasant memory of Hawkes, Scroby reached his own door without further trouble and placed the key accurately in the lock. Wilkins should make him a cup of coffee to clear his head and then he would have a bath and go to bed. Damnation, of course Wilkins was out for the night to see his sister at Dorking. Menservants shouldn't have sisters at Dorking. Irritation brought on Scroby's malaise again and he clung to the doorpost with one hand, groping for the electric light switch

9

with the other. Somebody had moved the damn thing, where was it? If Wilkins had been in, the lights would have been on. Been in, been on. In, on. Out, off. Simple. But Wilkins would be back early in the morning because Aunt Angela was coming to lunch and everything must be just so.

The room was not dark since the blinds had not been drawn, and the street lights outside illuminated the place quite clearly; one could see all the furniture and even that there were pictures on the walls. There were the locked cabinets containing his collection of snuffboxes and the Buhl clock on the mantelpiece. Something strange on that low table. Of course, that damned awful great Japanese vase Aunt Angela gave him which only came out when she was coming and lived in a cupboard between visits. Wilkins must have put it out ready for the morning. Scroby averted his eyes from the dim shape of Aunt Angela's vase and saw something else instead.

Something even stranger and far more menacing, a large lump upon the sill of one of his windows. The lump rose higher and became the head and shoulders of a man. Also the window, a little open at top and bottom on that warm night, opened slowly and silently wider.

Scroby was not normally in the habit of doing things for himself. "Why," he was in the habit of saying, "keep a dog and bark yourself?" Normally, his reaction to the sight of a burglar upon his windowsill would be to ring down to the office and say: "There is a burglar upon my windowsill. Kindly arrange for his immediate removal." He would then, normally, draw the curtains in the burglar's face and sit down quietly with a book until the resultant clamor had ceased, but this evening was not normal. He felt ill and unsteady, there was no one to make him coffee or draw his bath, and now there was this intruder come to exasperate him.

Scroby suddenly lost his temper. He walked silently across the thick carpet and picked up the Japanese vase by its long neck. By this time the burglar had his hands inside the room and, his elbows on the sill, he heaved himself up and put his head in through the open window.

Scroby took the heavy vase back over his shoulder and brought it down like a club on the man's head. There was a crash and a scatter of broken china, a muffled cry as the burglar disappeared, and a nasty thud on the concrete road below. There were also moaning sounds, but Scroby was not interested.

"Now, at last," he said aloud, "I shall be able to go to bed."

He wandered off across the sitting room and into his bedroom, dropped his discarded clothes in disorder on the floor, crawled into his pajamas, climbed into bed, and was immediately asleep.

Half an hour later he was dragged up from immeasurable depths of slumber by someone shaking his shoulder; when he opened his eyes there was a light shining straight into them. Most painful. He covered his face with his hands, rolled over on the pillow, and snarled: "Go away."

His bedside light, a decorously shaded affair, was switched on and a firm but kindly voice was telling him to wake up. "Please wake up, sir. I am so sorry, but you really must wake up."

Scroby said: "Oh, hell," in a dreary voice and opened his eyes to see a policeman in uniform at the side of his bed. Curiosity roused him and he asked what the policeman wanted at that hour of the night.

"It's about a burglar, sir. Did you have a burglar in your flat tonight?"

"Burglar," said Scroby, thinking back. "You mean the man on my windowsill, do you? He didn't say he was a burglar."

"They don't, sir, as a rule."

"Oh, don't they? Well, he didn't, either." Scroby slid down in the bed and pulled the sheet over his face, but the policeman uncovered it again and persevered.

"If you would be so good as to give me a short account of what happened—"

Scroby uttered a noise which was so like a moo that the policeman, who had been brought up on a farm, reverted automatically to the days of his youth.

"Co-oop," he said sympathetically, "co-oop, then. Sorry, sir."

Scroby was touched.

"Listen, officer. I've shpent—spent—the evening at a perfectly foul dinner in a fug you could chop with a knife, drinking about three times more than I wanted to with a gang of old-school hearties I never wish to see again. I've got a thick head and my eyes hurt me and I wish I hadn't eaten the fish. Couldn't you, please, go away and come back in the morning? Oh, gosh, no, don't do that either, Aunt Angela's coming to lunch. Oh, why was I ever born?"

"What you want," said the policeman, "is a nice strong cup of coffee," and he left the room. When he came back ten minutes later he had, of course, to wake up Scroby again, but this time the coffee helped and the officer got his story.

"So I hit him and he disappeared," finished Scroby. "Then I went to bed."

"He fell down from the window, did he?"

"Now you mention it," said Scroby, scooping sugar out of the bottom of the cup with his spoon, "I do remember hearing a sort of thud."

"You didn't look out to see, sir?"

"Dear me, no. I hadn't wanted to see him the first time, why should I want to look at him again?"

The policeman turned over a page in his notebook.

"He broke his ankle," he said. "So we were called and we got him."

Scroby thought this over. The coffee was now getting to its work of stimulating his mental processes and it seemed to him that this statement, though admirably simple and clear, had some strange undercurrent of meaning. "We got him" was not how one would expect a policeman to describe his dealings with a man who had broken his ankle. "We got him into an ambulance" well and good, "We rushed him off to hospital" still better. But "We got him" in a tone of—yes, that was it, unmistakable triumph—

"Why?" said Scroby slowly. "Did you want him?"

"Want him!" said the constable, and laughed. "You wouldn't know who he was, I suppose? That was Toni Le Chat, that was. Remember that double murder in Highgate ten days ago? Old chap and his wife lived over a little antique shop. This Toni Le Chat got in the bathroom window and brained them both, and we've been looking for him ever since. He had two or three pals with him, but we don't know so much about them."

"Do you mean to tell me that that man at my window was a brutal murderer?"

"That's right."

Scroby began to laugh. "And I dotted him one with Aunt Angela's— ha, ha-ha—Aunt Angela's Japanese vase—oh, ha-ha, ha, ho-ho—Aunt Angela—"

"Here," said the policeman, "what you want is a nice drop of brandy. Where d'you keep it?"

Scroby stopped laughing abruptly.

"No, thank you, officer. Even the smell of it, tonight—no, thank you."

"Well, I'll leave you now, and thank you, sir. You understand you may have to give evidence at the magistrate's court of the incidents leading up to the arrest?"

"Oh, shall I?"

"Yes, sir. But possibly not at the trial, because if they can make that murder case stick, they won't bother about a mere attempted burglary."

"No, I see. No, I shouldn't, in their place. Oh lord, whatever will Aunt Angela say?"

The policeman put his notebook in his pocket and rose to go.

"About your front door, sir, I found it standing open. Will you lock it after me?"

"Just shut it, officer. I'll lock up in a minute."

But before the front door closed behind the policeman, Scroby was asleep again.

Another half hour passed and Scroby gradually became if not awake at least partly conscious. Something had disturbed him. His subliminal consciousness, having been alarmed by midnight tales of burglary and murder, was on the watch though the rest of Scroby was profoundly asleep. There were sounds of people moving about in his sitting room and even two or three momentary but brilliant flashes of light. Scroby's subliminal consciousness knocked and told him about it.

"Nonsense," said Scroby's waking brain. "It's only Wilkins tidying up. He'll be in with my tea in a minute." But a nagging doubt persisted and Scroby opened one eye to discover that darkness still reigned about the Meridian of Greenwich. It was not, therefore, Wilkins, who was doubtless still snoring peacefully at Dorking, but some other intruder. The bedroom door was ajar as the policeman had left it, and there were lights on in the sitting room.

Scroby set his teeth. He had the law-abiding Englishman's respect for the police and he was a considerate man by nature, but if this were some more of the Metropolitan Constabulary still bumbling about his flat in the small hours, they should hear something to their advantage, by heck they should. As he rolled over and switched on the bedside light the door opened and two men looked in. They were not in uniform; they were hatless and wore loose raincoats over baggy suits. Detectives, presumably.

"Now look here," said Scroby indignantly. "I've told your constable what happened and he wrote it all down. Can't you all go back to Scotland Yard together and let him read it out to you?"

The men smiled amiably.

"We aren't detectives, sir," said the first man rapidly, "we are Press. Daily *Megaphone*, sir, Breezy News for Bright People; my name's Morgan, here's my card." He advanced with swift strides to lay a card on the bedside table and Scroby saw with unmitigated horror that the second man had a camera.

"I won't be photographed, I tell you, I will not, take that thing outside—"

"That's all right, sir. No photos without permission. Would you care to give us a few words about what happened tonight?"

"No, I wouldn't. I hate publicity, I don't want to talk, I've nothing to tell you, I've got a headache— Oh, go away!"

"But the news—"

"Damn the news! I'm not interested. I read *The Times—*"

"But, sir, you are news, whether you like it or not. You're the man who threw Tony the Cat out of a first-floor window—"

"Cat? It was a man, not a cat. I wouldn't—"

"Tony the Cat. Toni le Chat, French. The murderer the police have been hunting, and you—"

"I didn't throw him out. He wasn't in. That is, he stuck his head in from outside."

The photographer pulled out of his pocket a long limp object which was in fact a nylon stocking and began to polish the big lens of his Linhoff camera.

"I see," said Morgan. "He was climbing in the window from outside and you pushed him off."

"Not pushed. I hit him with a vase and he fell down. That's all."

"I see. And the vase broke, the pieces are on the floor, aren't they?" Scroby closed his eyes and shuddered and Morgan spoke to the photographer. "Horace, a shot of those pieces."

The photographer pushed his odd stocking carelessly into his pocket and went out; a moment or two later there was a bright flicker from the sitting room.

"And what did you do then, sir? Summon the police?"

"No. I went to bed."

"You looked out of the window, I take it, sir?"

"No. I went to bed," said Scroby irritably. "I was tired so I went straight to bed. What's the matter with that?"

"Well—"

"And now I should like to go to sleep. Would you very kindly have the infinite politeness to Go Away?"

"Very good, sir," said Morgan, shutting up his notebook and retiring. "I've got my story, anyway."

There followed a few low-toned remarks from the sitting room which Scroby could not and did not wish to hear and presently the outer door closed. Scroby dragged himself out of bed, staggered out to the front door and locked it, disentangled his foot from the photographer's stocking which had been dropped on the carpet, tottered back again and fell into bed.

He was gently and discreetly awakened by the sound of a china tray being set down on the bedside table and the refined swish of a blind being pulled up. The sun was streaming into the room, the air was fresh, and there was Wilkins' deferential voice asking: "Shall I pour out your tea, sir?"

Scroby sat up. He had a dim recollection of having had a disturbed night, a bad dream, probably. He disregarded it because obviously all was well on this lovely morning. Wilkins moved about the room tidying away the garments strewn about the floor and Scroby drank his tea. As he turned to set down his cup, a card on the bedside table caught his eye. "J. Morgan. *Daily Megaphone. Breezy News for Bright People.*" It was not a bad dream, it was all true; like a tidal wave, it swept over him, the burglar, the vase, Aunt Angela—

"Wilkins," he said, and his voice croaked like one of Macbeth's gloomier ravens, "Wilkins, where are the papers?"

"The Times, sir, and the Daily *Telegraph* are close by your left hand as usual, sir."

Scroby skimmed hastily through headlines and found nothing to startle or offend the most sensitive reader.

"Wilkins. Go out and get me a copy of the Daily *Megaphone,* will you?"

"I have already obtained a copy, sir."

Wilkins left the room and returned at once with a newspaper which counterbalanced its smaller size with its larger—much larger—headlines. He held it out to Scroby in such a way that the full impact could be felt at once.

TONI LE CHAT CAPTURED.
CLUBMAN FELLS HIM WITH VASE.
"I MERELY WENT STRAIGHT TO BED."

Richard Scroby, well known to connoisseurs as a collector of snuffboxes, described to our representative how he foiled an attempt—

Master and man stared wildly into each other's face for a long minute. "Er—precisely, sir," said Wilkins.

CHAPTER II
One Nylon Stocking

WHILE SCROBY was having his bath the front doorbell rang and Wilkins answered it. It rang again and Wilkins answered it. Again and the same again.

Scroby was mildly puzzled. If there were callers he would have expected Wilkins to come and tell him about them; surely they could not all have come to the wrong number? He cut short his customary wallow, omitted his morning calisthenics, and came out.

"Wilkins? What was all that?"

"Merely persons representing the Press, sir." Wilkins advanced with a salver upon which lay several cards bearing well-known names.

"Oh, gosh. What did you tell them?"

"That after a disturbed night, sir, you were not prepared to give so early an audience."

"Good."

"I added, sir, that the matter being obviously *subjudice,* it was possible that you might not feel yourself at liberty to speak about the affair at all."

"Excellent. What did they say to that?"

"Er—'apple sauce,' sir, was the usual riposte."

"Oh."

Scroby went into his bedroom and proceeded to dress. All this was most disturbing but only needed to be firmly handled. Probably the most effective way would be for him to type out a brief statement in triplicate or quadruplicate or even quintuplicate; that ought to be enough. The appropriate word for sixfold persistently eluded him and in any case his typewriter would not endure the production of 1 + 5 copies. He tied his tie while composing half a dozen brief but explicit sentences. No fancy writing, no adjectives; a plain dignified narrative. "I entered my flat and put down my hat and immediately saw what was not there before, a man on the sill. I crept forward until I was well within reach. I thought I would teach him to let me alone—alone—phone—disown—

"I am *not* writing doggerel," he said angrily, aloud. "Or am I? Not like that at all. Plain and dignified. 'I saw a man at my window, he was trying to lift the sash, I did not desire him to enter, I foiled him by making a dash.' What the hell's the matter with me this morning? It can't still be the port."

The front doorbell rang again and kept on ringing. Brushing noises in the sitting room, where Wilkins was clearing up, ceased. The next moment the bell ceased also, for Wilkins had opened the door. Scroby paused, hairbrush in hand, and listened. There were voices; Wilkins had admitted someone. A female voice, growing momentarily louder as the speaker advanced across the room. Scroby tottered towards the bed and sat down upon it. Wilkins tapped at the door and entered.

"Miss Scroby, sir."

"I know. I heard her. Wilkins, what is the time?"

"Nine twenty-seven, sir."

"Thank you. Shut the door and come here. Wilkins, am I in the habit of lunching at 9:30 A.M.?"

"Not since I have been in your service, sir."

"Nor before. My compliments to Miss Scroby and I shall be delighted to see her at 1:15 P.M. as arranged."

"Excuse me, sir—"

"Well?"

"She is carrying a copy of the *Daily Megaphone,* sir."

Scroby turned upon him large and liquid eyes as full of the sadness of this suffering world as those of a spaniel whose master is not taking him out.

"Further, sir, I was in the act of clearing up the broken china. Not expecting Miss Scroby, I left it still in view, in the dustpan, sir."

"She has seen it."

"Yes, sir. Further yet—"

"Wilkins, there can be nothing further."

"There is the stocking, sir."

"Stocking? What do you mean, stocking?"

"One stocking, sir, nylon. Somewhat the worse for wear, sir."

"Wilkins, I swear by whatever you hold most holy that I am completely innocent of stockings. Where did it come from—Ah! Is it one of your sister's whom—I mean, which—you inadvertently caught up in mistake for a handkerchief this morning? It must be."

"My sister, sir, wears only lisle thread. But, now you suggest it, Miss Scroby does not know my sister. Leave the stocking to me, sir."

"With the utmost confidence, Wilkins. I have quite enough to explain away without becoming entangled in stockings. See if you can shunt her off till a more reasonable hour."

"I will try, sir," said Wilkins in a doubtful voice.

"Do so."

Wilkins left the room and Scroby dispiritedly resumed his toilet, but the joyous mood of the morning had fled. The chirping of the London sparrows was an insult, the brilliant sunshine mocked him, the cloudless blue sky was most unsympathetic. He sighed deeply and went to listen at the door; there was no sound of voices and where Aunt Angela was there was usually the sound of at least one voice. Wilkins had got rid of her, then. Excellent man, Wilkins. Scroby cheered up perceptibly and opened the door to admit the lovely aroma of coffee and grilled bacon. Life, after all, had its splendid moments. Humming a carefree stave from the opera *Rigoletto,* he strode into the room.

"Richard!"

Scroby and his song stopped abruptly as a small gray lady rose from the recesses of his largest armchair.

"Oh—ah—hello, Aunt Angela."

"Good morning, Richard."

She held up her left cheek and he saluted her in the approved manner.

"Good morning, Aunt Angela. How well you look, but then you always do. You know, you do surprise me, seeing you here, I mean. You know, I had an idea I'd asked you to lunch, not breakfast, though of course you are always most welcome, as you know, and no doubt if there is any mistake in the appointment it is I who have made it, not you, most careless of me, I do apologize and it won't take Wilkins a moment to grill some more bacon. Wilkins! Lay another place for Miss Scroby. The only trouble is—"

"I breakfasted an hour and a half ago, Richard, thank you—"

"Oh, then you're about ready for another, so Wilkins can carry on. The trouble is—"

"I should be glad of a cup of coffee but no more, thank you."

Scroby hurried across to the pantry door, put his head in and said: "A cup of coffee and no more, thank you. A cup of coffee and no more, thank you. A cup—"

"One moment, sir," said Wilkins, and Scroby by some miracle found himself inside the pantry with the door shut and Wilkins practically holding a glass to his lips. Scroby swallowed it and immediately warmth returned to his limbs and calm to his brain. He drew a long breath.

"Thank you, Wilkins."

"Thank you, sir. I will bring the breakfast in a moment."

"What was that I swallowed?"

"A small dose of cognac, sir. It settles the stomach."

"I wish it would settle my aunt too," said Scroby, but he threw his shoulders back and returned to his guest.

"Please forgive me, Aunt Angela. An order I had omitted to give Wilkins. Well now, the trouble is that I have only just time to bolt my breakfast before I rush off to see my man of business."

Miss Scroby took no notice.

"I came up to town early in order to do some shopping before lunch and in my hurry to catch the eight-ten I left my *Daily Telegraph* behind, so I bought another paper at the station bookstall to read in the train. Richard, it was this."

She confronted him with the front page of the *Daily Megaphone*.

"Not at all your type, Aunt Angela—"

"I was led by Providence. There is no doubt in my mind about it, otherwise I should probably never have known that you, my nephew and a Scroby, had been associated in the public press with burglars and murderers."

"Only one, Aunt—"

"Only one? Is not one enough?"

"Oh, quite. I only meant that they were the same man. I mean, there was only one of him. I mean—"

"I know quite well what you mean, Richard. I have read the article myself."

Wilkins came in with a tray: coffee, bacon, and toast.

"I think I've lost my appetite, Wilkins."

"Let me pour you a cup of coffee, sir. Try to drink it, sir, the effects are said to be restorative. Madam takes milk and sugar?"

"Both, Wilkins, thank you. Richard, why should a healthy young man of your age require a restorative in the morning?"

"I've no idea, Aunt Angela. Why should he?"

"I meant you."

"You meant me," murmured Scroby, and gazed vaguely into infinity.

"Your coffee, sir," urged Wilkins.

"Oh, thank you," said Scroby, and drank it straight off. "Another cup, please."

"Tell me, Richard, why did you grant an interview in the middle of the night to a sensational rag like the *Megaphone?* Why the *Megaphone?* When your dear grandfather was elected Mayor *honoris causa* of Scroby-with-Scattering in 1894 he gave an interview to a representative of *The Times,* though by some misunderstanding it was inadvertently omitted from publication. Why did you not select a paper of good standing such—"

"Because the *Megaphone* was here and all the other papers weren't. I mean, none of the other papers were."

"A small rasher of bacon, sir," said Wilkins, lifting a silver lid.

"Wilkins," said Miss Scroby, "why are you hovering round Mr. Scroby as though he were an invalid? There's nothing the matter with him, is there?"

"I trust not, madam." Wilkins laid two rashers reverently upon Scroby's plate and withdrew.

"And the vase," said Miss Scroby. "Why did you break that valuable vase?"

"I wanted something to hit the burglar with."

"But why the vase? Have you not—"

"No fire-irons. Electric fires don't have fire-irons. I never thought of that before, Aunt Angela, but it's quite true. Can I give you a little more coffee?"

"No, thank you. Richard. How old are you?"

Scroby considered. "Twenty-three, I think. Aren't I?"

"You ought to be married."

"No, thank you. I—"

"You want someone to look after you."

"I've got Wilkins."

"I mean someone"—she glanced round but the pantry door was shut—"someone of your own class who would have a good and steadying influence upon you." Scroby shuddered. "There is my goddaughter Millicent Biggleswade, the Rector's daughter. You used to play so prettily together when you were children; surely you remember her."

"Is that the girl with a face like a suet pudding?"

"Richard. She is a dear good girl and plays the piano quite beautifully."

"I remember. She was sick at my birthday party."

"She is fond of poetry and arranges flowers quite exquisitely."

But Scroby was still resentful of a ruined festivity.

"She ate too much, Aunt Angela. She always did."

"Richard! She is Lord Welter's granddaughter."

Wilkins came through the sitting room on his way to Scroby's bedroom.

"Welter," said Scroby thoughtfully. "Somebody mentioned Welter to me the other day. Wilkins, it was you, wasn't it?"

"Yes, sir. I was in Lord Welter's service at one time."

"You have been in good service, Wilkins," said Miss Scroby kindly. "And yet you left him?"

"Yes, madam. That would be his present lordship, madam, naturally."

"Of course. A charming family."

Scroby suddenly remembered what he had been told.

"Did you find him so, Wilkins?"

"A little difficult at times, sir. A tendency to throw his boots. At first the habit could be overlooked, but unfortunately his aim improved with practice, so I resigned my post, sir."

"But, Wilkins, you cannot mean that his lordship threw his boots at you?"

"Not intentionally, madam. His lordship used to mistake me for a pink elephant."

Wilkins bowed slightly and moved off, closing the bedroom door behind him.

"I do feel," said Scroby earnestly, "that, dear good girl as Millicent is, her heredity leaves something to be desired. These old families—"

"Nonsense, Richard. This is the present Earl he's talking about. He gets it from his mother's side. Nothing to do with Millicent."

"I don't care," said Scroby, turning at bay. "I don't like Millicent."

Miss Scroby unmasked her last battery.

"Then why the stocking?"

"Stocking? What stocking?"

"You are blushing, Richard. Do not deny it. Indeed, I am glad to see it if it may be taken as a sign of grace."

Scroby silently cursed his overenergetic bloodstream which at school had earned him the name of Beetroot.

"I don't know anything about it. Probably Wilkins—"

"Wilkins told me a cock-and-bull story about its being an old one of his sister's he uses for cleaning."

"Well, there you—"

"Nonsense. A woman of the type of Wilkins' sister to wear an expensive nylon stocking embroidered with cupid's hearts? Don't be ridiculous, Richard."

"But I—"

"You are running into evil courses, Richard, and I owe it to the Scrobys to check it in the bud. What you want, as I said just now, is a sensible levelheaded wife. You had better come back with me and stay with me for a few weeks and then we shall see."

Scroby was terrified of his aunt, but the primeval instinct of self-preservation will make even a cornered rabbit turn.

"I won't marry," he said. "I should simply hate it."

"That's silly, Richard. How can you know you don't like marriage when you've never tried it?"

"I am very happy as I am and I don't propose to change."

Miss Scroby sighed deeply.

"Then there is only one thing for it. I must immolate myself."

"But, Aunt Angela," said the horrified Scroby, "I can't marry you, it isn't allowed. It's within the whatsies—you know—A Man May Not Marry His Grandmother."

"Idiot! I wouldn't marry you if you were no relation at all and the last man alive. No. I see my duty plain and, painful as it is, I shall perform it."

"Aunt Angela—"

"It will break my heart and you will never appreciate the sacrifice, but I will do it."

"For heaven's sake, what?"

"I shall sell my dear little cottage at Marsh Mooring and come and live in the next flat above here. The porter told me this morning that it was to be vacant; I now realize that this is providential."

"No, no," said Scroby passionately, "I will not allow it, I—"

The clamor of the front doorbell drowned his low and trembling voice; before Wilkins could reach the door it rang again and even as he laid his hand upon the doorhandle the knocker sounded. Wilkins opened the door to admit a representative of the *London Daily Record,* that great paper; the architect-in-charge of the block of flats to inspect the scene of the outrage; a young man with a large cardboard box from Scroby's tailor; and a policeman in uniform.

Scroby rose to his feet and looked wildly round him.

"I shan't detain you a moment, sir," said the *Record* man. "If I could have just a few words?"

"I needn't bother you at all," said the architect, "if I might just have a look at this window. Which one was it, this?"

"No, that—"

"Sign for the parcel, please," said the young man to Wilkins. " 'Ere's a pencil."

"A message for you, sir," said the policeman. "We shall not require to trouble you to attend the magistrate's court—"

"Thank goodness for the first cheerful thing I've had said to me this morning!"

"If you would be so good as to read through this statement and, if you consider it to be an accurate record of your statement made at 1 A.M. today, will you please sign it?"

"It's that down-pipe there," said the architect.

"Not on that line, the one above, look," said the young man.

"How did it begin?" asked the *Record* man. "Were you sitting in here, sir? I assume that the lights were not on?"

"I am going," said Miss Scroby. "*Au revoir,* Richard."

"I expect you've got some shopping to do, haven't you? Will you be back to lunch?"

"Not shopping, Richard. Inspecting flats."

"Is that really your name, sir?" said the policeman. "I thought it was Scroby, sir."

"What? Oh hell!"

"Yes, sir. I thought that couldn't be right."

One by one the visitors departed and at last Scroby was alone.

"Wilkins."

"Sir?"

"This won't do. I'm steadily going mad. Did you hear Miss Scroby saying that she was going to take the flat above this?"

"I gathered that Madam had some such intention, sir."

"And I can't stop her!"

"No, sir. Excuse me, there is an alternative. We could go somewhere else, sir."

Scroby's face lit up.

"I understand, sir, that the accommodation known as Albany is not available to the female sex."

"In that case there won't be a vacancy for fifty years. But we might go somewhere else."

"Yes, sir. The photographers and the other journalists spoke of returning later, sir."

Scroby bounded from his chair.

"Pack my things, Wilkins. We are leaving at once."

"In order to make a suitable selection, may I ask where we intend going?"

"To Cornwall, of course. Where I always go. They know me there, they'll find me a room. Why are you shaking your head like that, Wilkins? You like Cornwall, don't you?"

"A pleasant and picturesque district, sir, but still within the reach of reporters. Though I understand that the local inhabitants deny that Corn-wall is a part of England, for practical purposes the frontier is nonexist-ent, sir."

"You think they'd chase me down there?"

"Certainly, sir. May I be permitted to suggest Paris?"

"Paris? But I've never been there."

"An exhilarating city, sir."

"Oh?" said Scroby, without much enthusiasm. "I take it you've been there, have you?"

"Oh yes, sir. Several of my gentlemen made a practice of going to Paris once or twice a year. A most interesting city, sir, with many muse-ums and galleries full of the most exquisite examples of the painter's and sculptor's art, sir. Also many historic buildings."

"Yes, that sounds all right, but I don't know that I'm much attracted. When I went to Scheveningen with the Marshalls two years ago I was bored stiff."

"So I recall, sir, but on that occasion it rained all the time and there are other differences. Our passports, sir, are still valid. Besides—" Wilkins paused.

"Besides what?"

"Paris would be a wonderful place for snuffboxes, sir. The antique shops of Paris are amongst the finest in Europe."

"Oh, are they? That is a consideration. Now I come to think of it, I met a man last night who lives in Paris. He was in my form at school, not a bad fellow. Writes for the papers about Paris and what goes on there. Man named Hawkes, he gave me his card, I suppose I've still got it."

"On your dressing table, sir," said Wilkins, and went to fetch it.

"It's got his Paris telephone number, yes. I'll ring him up and ask him to recommend a hotel."

"But if he is in London, sir—"

"He was flying back early this morning. Wilkins, that's an idea. We also will fly. It is quicker. It is also appropriate. I feel I must fly; well, let us do so."

"Psychologically fitting, sir. Shall we be taking the car, sir?"

"What? Oh no. There are all sorts of formalities to go through when one takes a car abroad, aren't there? Triptyques, whatever they are. Be-sides, I've never driven abroad, have you?"

"Oh yes, sir. Many thousands of miles with some of my previous gentlemen, sir. I still have my International Driving License, sir, if required."

"Take it with you. If we want a car we can hire one and you can drive it. Now I'll get on to Hawkes while you pack. Hurry, Wilkins, hurry!"

"With pleasure, sir."

CHAPTER III
Séance

SCROBY and his manservant arrived at the air terminal near the Madeleine in the autobus which had brought them from Le Bourget and found Hawkes waiting for them.

"I say, Hawkes, this is extremely good of you—"

"Not at all, only unfortunately I haven't a moment to spare. Hi, taxi! I've found you a hotel, I'll just go along with you and then I must dash off to a meeting. Is this luggage all yours? I say, how much excess did you have to pay? Hôtel de la Lune d'Italie, please. You've got some rather splendid ideas about accommodation, haven't you? Bedroom and sitting room with a spare bedroom for a manservant and all the other doings *en suite;* the management thought you must be a honeymoon couple. Look, Scroby, I'm frightfully busy but I will take time to show you some of the better bits of Paris in a day or two. Oh, by the way, I've got an assignment for tonight, got to look up a spiritualist medium they think is phony. I've got two tickets, would you care to come along? Do, I think it may be fun. Well, look, I'll call for you at half-past nine, see how you feel about it then. Here's your hotel. Porter, this is Monsieur Scroby and his man, they are having that suite I booked today. I must rush, I'm late already. See you at nine-thirty."

"Th-thank you so much," said Scroby breathlessly, but Hawkes was already out of sight.

"A very sudden gentleman, sir," said Wilkins.

"He's a newspaperman," said Scroby, "that's all. I have met them before—before last night, I mean. Wilkins, we are here. We have escaped."

"Yes, sir. Excuse me, sir. The porter is addressing you. He is suggesting that he should take us up to our rooms, sir."

"Good idea," said Scroby amiably. "*Allez.* Or is it *allons?*"

"This way, sir," said the porter, "to the lift. It is here. Please, sir, after you. This is all the luggage, yes? Good, very good. This lift, it works itself on applying oneself to the button, you see? One for first floor, two for second floor, and so on up. Monsieur is on the first floor, so, and the lift stops himself. All right, yes?"

"Splendid," said Scroby. "I know these lifts, I have one like this at home."

"Splendid," said the porter, who continually strove to enlarge his vocabulary. "Monsieur will therefore feel at home here, eh? Along here, on the left, the numbers four, five, and six. Four is your sitting room, five your bedroom, and six your man's room." He threw open doors one after the other and hustled the luggage inside. "All right, eh? I leave you now; you come down just whenever you are ready, and register in the office. Anything you want, you lift the telephone and I am on the other end. All right? Splendid." He smiled and nodded and went out, shutting the doors behind him.

Scroby took his hat off, threw it on a table, and stood looking about him. The rooms were good-class hotel rooms; that is, they contained everything one could reasonably need and nothing that one would remember the day after leaving them.

"Is everything satisfactory, sir?" asked Wilkins.

"What? Oh yes, thanks, perfectly. Wilkins, was Miss Scroby coming back to lunch or was she not?"

"I was uncertain, sir. I therefore left a message with the hall porter of our flats that we had been suddenly called away on business and that no doubt you would be communicating with her in due course, sir."

"Did you say we were going to Paris?"

"Oh no, sir," said Wilkins in a shocked voice. "It would not have been my place, sir."

"Thank you, Wilkins."

"Thank you, sir."

Three men were sitting round a table in a quiet corner of a café and talking earnestly together over their drinks.

"So we are in Paris again in safety," said Pépi, called The Crocodile. "I hate London; I am always glad to come away."

"I am not. Not this time. I think you a fool, Pépi, to come running back here so soon. There was that little job in Cripplegate; easy, quick, and would have paid us well. Who would have expected to see such diamonds in so small a place? But you would go, and Fingers here would back you up. You are wrong, I tell you."

"No," said Fingers Dupré, and lit another cigarette.

"It would only have meant one more evening," persisted Jules. "It was all set out and laid on, couldn't go wrong."

Pépi made a rude noise conveying incredulity. "That flat job after the snuffboxes, that was all laid on too. Couldn't that go wrong? Couldn't it?"

"So what? We weren't inside, were we? Nobody saw us, did they? Nobody about, was there? Yet if I hadn't had the sense to grab Toni's wallet off him before we cleared out, we'd have had nothing. Nothing! Yet when I remind you there's that Cripplegate stuff just waiting for us to pick it up, you can't wait a few hours to do it. Windy, that's what you are."

Pépi emptied his glass, set it down, and leaned across the table.

"Listen, Jules. You don't know English law but I do. I have been in England before, as you know, and I can speak and read English. Those two old dodderers Toni knocked off at Highgate. Well, that's murder."

"I know that, but Toni did it, not us, and they've got him."

"But we were outside, and in English law, Jules, the ones outside are just as guilty as the one inside, because they are helping him. Accessory-before-the-fact, they call it. We were helping Toni so we are for arrest and trial—"

"Idiot!" raged Jules, banging the table with his fist. "Fool! I never even saw the two old—!"

"I know," insisted Pépi, "but it's murder all the same. What is more, if they follow us up and recognize us, the English will apply for our extra-dition, and back we go to take what's coming to us. Now can you see why I think we ought to get down to Marseilles and not stop in Paris?"

Jules thought this over, but the taciturn Dupré for once had some-thing to say.

"Not just now," he said. "Tourist season beginning," for he owed his nickname of Fingers to the fact that he was a pickpocket. "Paris better than Marseilles. But—"

Pépi interrupted him. "Listen again, Jules. You think Toni was just unlucky, don't you?"

"Somebody slipped up," agreed Jules. "We was told they was both going to be out, the fat valet away for the night and the boss out at a dinner till late. But he must have come home early, so Toni was unlucky, that is true."

"No," said Pépi.

"No?"

"No. It was not bad luck, it was a trap. Listen again. There was no light in that window, was there, when Toni put his head in? We were watching and there was no light. Yet Scroby was there waiting. I tell you, he was police and he was waiting. It was a trap, I tell you. Even after Toni fell down there was still no light in the window. Why? Because he had dodged out again to call up his friends. You, Jules, you only had bare time to take Toni's wallet and run for it before the police were there. I tell you, he had them ready waiting. He is police, I tell you."

"That is why—" began Fingers Dupré, but the other two did not heed him.

"Toni said," continued Pépi, "that he found it easy to make the fat servant talk in that café where all the menservants go. Of course the servant talked; he'd been told to, I say."

"Even so," persisted Jules, "they do not know about us. We were not staying together in London. We only met sometimes and then with every care."

"Sometimes! Every day, and sometimes more often. You do not know who sees you in London. I do not like the place. One feels, all the time, that there are eyes on one's back. Toni has a broken ankle, but presently they will take him and break his neck. That Scroby, he was police."

"That is why he is here," said Fingers, and the other two turned upon him.

"Here? Where? What d'you mean?"

"Here, in Paris. I saw him today."

"You are being stupid," said Jules.

"You have made a mistake," said Pépi, but without confidence.

"No. I was at the air terminal to see who came. He got out." Fingers emptied his glass and looked at it mournfully.

"A moment," said Pépi, and snapped his fingers for the waiter.

"The same again," said Pépi, and they all sat in silence till the waiter came back with the refilled glasses.

"Now, Fingers," said Pépi. "You are perfectly certain that it was he and no other?"

"Certain. We saw him often when we were watching the flats, did we not?"

"Toni pointed him out to us," agreed Jules. "And the servant also."

"He came this afternoon," said Fingers.

"And what happened?"

"Man waiting for them. Taxi to hotel."

"Them?" said Jules. "Is the servant here too?"

Fingers nodded and sipped his wine.

"Fingers," said Pépi. "I suppose you were not able to hear what hotel they were going to?"

"La Lune d'Italie."

"Well done," said Pépi, but Dupré's impassive face showed neither pleasure nor triumph nor any other emotion and there was a long pause.

"Fingers," said Jules. "He doesn't—he didn't know you, did he?"

"Don't think so. No."

"There's only two ways out of it," said Pépi. "Either we go to Marseilles, or—"

"What's to stop him going to Marseilles too?" said Jules.

"I tell you," said Pépi, "either we go to Marseilles or he goes to the police."

Dupré turned down his thumbs.

"I agree," said Jules. "In the Seine, with a weight to keep him down."

"But that's murder again," said Pépi.

"He should have stayed in London, then," said Jules. "It is his fault."

At half-past nine that night Hawkes came to the Hotel of the Moon of Italy and found Scroby waiting for him.

"That's good," said Hawkes. "It isn't far, we'll walk, shall we? Right, let's go."

"I should like to walk," said Scroby, "with someone who knows where he is going and how to get there. I went out for a stroll myself soon after we arrived, but it was all a bit confusing. Very interesting, of course, but I didn't know where I was, so I bought some street maps and went back again. I do feel I know a little more now. That imposing building at the end of this street is the Madeleine, is it?"

"Try again," said Hawkes. "That's the Opera House. Never mind. Scroby, this affair we are going to is a séance. Have you ever been to a séance before?"

"Never. Don't they wave white muslin and throw flour about?"

"That does happen sometimes, but I don't know whether it will to-night. This woman—the medium—was operating in London and though I don't think anyone actually caught her out in anything she was given to understand that it would be awfully nice of her to go away. Right away, somewhere outside the U.K. So she came to Paris."

"What nationality is she, then?"

"Heaven knows. She may even be French. So I am going to her show tonight to see if there is any funny business going on, if I can, though some of these people are quite clever."

"I'm afraid I'm not terribly good at anything like this," said Scroby frankly. "I mean, I never have the foggiest idea how these fellows do conjuring tricks. I know they're all tricks—I mean, billiard balls don't come out of the air—but they're much too clever for me. Hadn't you better take someone a bit more on the spot than I am if you want any help with your detecting?"

"My dear chap! I'm not a detective and I don't want any help. I'm only a poor benighted journalist trying to get material for an article, heaven help me. No, I only suggested you should come along for an amusing evening. Look, Scroby, if you get bored just slide out, don't wait for me."

"All right. But I don't expect I shall be bored, I never am. Even that old-school dinner last night wasn't boring, it was only that I felt so rotten."

"So you sensibly went home and got there in time to floor a burglar with a plated entree-dish or something; I read about it in the paper on my way over. Stout effort."

"Oh, it was nothing," said Scroby, who had no wish to be reminded of that from which he was escaping. "Tell me what you do, are you on the staff of some paper?"

"Yes, the *London Record*. I write mainly articles about life in Paris, all that sort of thing. We cross the road here and turn left—*Look out!* Scroby, you must remember that they drive on the right in France."

"I know, I know," said Scroby penitently. "Stupid of me. I nearly got run over when I was out before."

"What happened? Now we can cross—come on."

"A gendarme spoke to me," said Scroby, trotting obediently at Hawkes' heels. "Are they all gendarmes?"

"The traffic cops are not gendarmes actually, they are called *agents de police*. It doesn't matter; whichever they are, you do what they say. What did he say?"

"I didn't catch it all but it must have been funny because people laughed."

"I daresay. Scroby, you speak French, do you?"

"Well, we learned it at school," said Scroby doubtfully.

"Oh. Well, you'll soon pick it up. Here we are, I think this is the right place. Yes. Well, here we go. *Allons, mes braves.*"

"*Allons,*" said Scroby smartly.

They entered what appeared to be the hall of a private house and Hawkes gave his cards of admission to an elderly maid of severe aspect in a black dress and a white cap and apron. Scroby, who had scarcely seen such things except in pre-first-war copies of *Punch,* smiled shyly at her and received no encouragement at all. She indicated a row of pegs, most of which already had coats hanging upon them; they hung up theirs also and were then ushered into a dimly lighted room where people were already sitting round a long table.

There did not appear to be two vacant seats together anywhere and in the rather church-like atmosphere of the meeting it did not seem fitting to ask anyone to move. Besides, there was no object in it. Scroby took a chair near the door and Hawkes passed him to sit about halfway along the table. Three more people came in almost at once and all the places were filled. There were several men present, but the majority of the company were women, as Scroby noticed with some uneasiness. He associated psychic phenomena with hysteria. What did one do if a lady went into hysterics? Pour water over her? No, of course not, one rose quietly to one's feet and unostentatiously left the room; Hawkes wouldn't mind. Scroby reassured himself and began to look round the table, but the two heavily shaded wall lights gave so little illumination that it was not easy to distinguish faces unless one knew the person very well indeed. There was Hawkes, four seats away from him, but the rest of the company were a set of indiscernible features. There was soft music being played in the background somewhere, but at the moment when Scroby became really conscious of it, it stopped and a woman walked slowly into the room from a door at the far end. It was quite difficult to see her at all because she was dressed in some very dark color and only a large white face and two white hands floated towards the head of the table. Evidently there was an empty chair there because the woman sat down and addressed the meeting.

She spoke in French but very slowly and distinctly so that even Scroby gathered the gist of it. There were spirits all about us at all times and under favorable circumstances they were sometimes able to communicate with us. A séance was so arranged as to provide these favorable circumstances . . . etheric rays . . . helpful spirits and others less helpful . . . spirit controls . . . Scroby's attention wandered till it was recalled by a common movement; everyone had their hands clasped together and the address had turned into a prayer.

Then the dim wall lights went out and were replaced by a small blue bulb such as is used in sleeping-car compartments on night journeys. The room was practically dark and within a minute or so the voices began, various voices of all ages, and usually someone at the table answered if only by a sob.

It was more than a little uncanny; the skin prickled at the back of Scroby's neck and he wished he had not come. Also, the French now being spoken was too rapid for him to follow it and he had an uncomfortable feeling that someone was breathing softly behind him. Hawkes might be enjoying this, but a very little more of it would be quite enough for Richard Scroby.

Presently the medium changed her rapid idiomatic French for the slow and distinct manner in which she had spoken at the beginning of the séance. Just so, Scroby felt, would foreigners speak their own tongues to those whom they suspected of not being able easily to follow them. It had, Scroby realized, the desired effect upon him; he could follow this easily enough.

"Is there an Englishman present? Several, I think. Is there an Englishman here whose name is Scroby?"

Scroby started so violently that he almost fell from his chair. He heard himself saying, *"Oui. C'est moi,"* in a voice he did not recognize and he saw Hawkes, from his place four chairs away, lean forward and look towards him.

"There are two gentlemen here asking for you. They are here, I see them plainly. They are both large men; one is taller and leaner than the other, also a little younger, I think. They wear dress of an old fashion. Do you know who I mean? They died a long time ago, in—in—in 1870, they say. Do you know them?"

Scroby tried to say he did not, but his voice failed him. He made a croaking noise and then shook his head. Hawkes came to his support, for Scroby recognized the voice which asked: "What are their names?"

There was a short pause.

"Latin—Latter—Latterby—Latimer. James and Charles Latimer. They say that you have need of them."

Astonishment braced Scroby's vocal cords. "Me? Oh no. Why should I?"

Another short pause as though the question were being passed on and the answer awaited. Then—

"They say they do not know why you need their help. They have been told so, but not why."

"Oh," said Scroby faintly. "Oh."

"They say you will hear from them. That is all. They have gone away."

The séance came to an end soon after that and Hawkes and Scroby walked away together.

"Well?" said Scroby after a long pause. "Did you think she was a fraud?"

"I think she is very clever," said Hawkes.

CHAPTER IV
Joyeuse

"COME TO MY hotel," said Scroby, "and Wilkins will find us a drink."

"Thank you," said Hawkes, "it'll make a change from everlastingly sitting in cafés. Besides, if the two tall gentlemen in old-fashioned dress are going to call on you, it'll be only civil to be at home. Prepare to receive ghosts!"

"They didn't say they were coming to see me," said Scroby. "They said I should hear from them."

"Over the telephone? Scroby, how much of that did you swallow?"

Scroby thought this over.

"Hawkes, did you give her my name?"

"No. And the name I gave when I got the tickets was not my own. I didn't want her to know I was a journalist."

"Then how did she know mine?"

"There might be a simple explanation for that," said Hawkes. "She was in London for some time—I told you—she might have seen you somewhere and been told your name."

"Yes," said Scroby slowly, "I suppose she might."

"And the rest, of course, was pure bunkum."

"What, about the Latimers? Oh no, it isn't."

"What?" said Hawkes.

"That's what was so queer about it. James and Charles Latimer were ancestors of mine. Well, sort of ancestors; I'm not descended from them, but my mother was a Latimer from Virginia."

"Are you trying to tell me that John and Charles Latimer—"

"James and Charles—"

"—ever really existed?"

"Certainly they did," said Scroby. "There was a bit of a mystery about them and the story was handed down, you know how things get handed down in families—"

"Turn-up noses," suggested Hawkes.

"And after all, it isn't so long ago, 1870. It isn't a hundred years. There are plenty of people about now whose parents remembered the Franco-Prussian War."

"I suppose so. What was the mystery?"

"They disappeared and no one knew what had become of them."

"Were they American—yes, you said so—"

"One was. Charles Latimer was a Virginian and fought in the American Civil War. When the South was licked he came to England and stayed with his English cousin James Latimer, who lived near Manchester somewhere. I believe there are still Latimers at—at Didsbury, yes, but I don't know them. Well, in 1870 James and Charles went to France—I don't know why—and were never heard of again."

Hawkes thought this over and then made up his mind. He broke into a laugh.

"Jolly good leg-pull, Scroby. You know, I very nearly believed it."

"But it's true, Hawkes."

"Oh, come on!"

"I mean, I can't vouch personally for the truth of the story because naturally I wasn't born then, but it is true that that is the perfectly well authenticated story. I mean, enquiries were made at the time and for some time after, too. Naturally. I'm quite serious, Hawkes."

"Well, I'm damned! I thought you looked a bit green when we came out, I don't wonder. Look, Scroby, is this story well known? I mean, is she likely to have heard it?"

"Oh no. It isn't very interesting unless you're connected with it, and even then it isn't much of a story, is it? I haven't thought of it myself for years, why should I? And anyway, Hawkes, my name isn't Latimer and nobody now knows my mother; she's been dead nearly twenty years. Even I don't remember her. Why connect me with it? Here's the Lune d'Italie, come in and have a drink."

"Thank you. I could do with one. I say, Scroby, it almost looks as though the medium wasn't a fraud, doesn't it, unless there's some other explanation. There must be one. I don't believe in this kind of thing."

"I don't think I do, either, but I did find it a bit startling," said Scroby plaintively. "Come up and perhaps Wilkins will be able to explain it away. He has an answer for most things."

They sat in Scroby's sitting room and Wilkins poured wine into glasses, offered cigarettes and lit them.

"Wilkins," said Scroby, "it seems that I may shortly meet some of my ancestors."

Wilkins looked startled. "Sir? I understood you to be in perfect health, has any untoward event—"

"Oh, I don't mean I'm going to die. I'm perfectly well."

"I am relieved to hear it, sir."

"Thank you. I meant, merely, that a couple of ancestors are coming to see me."

"An elderly couple, sir?"

"Not as you mean it. Two men. They died in 1870."

Wilkins refilled their glasses. "Most interesting, sir. Will they be calling here, sir?"

"Wilkins," said Hawkes, "did you acquire that manner entirely by training or were you born like it?"

"It is largely a matter of practice, sir."

"But you must have a natural gift for it. I bet you didn't even yell when you were born."

"I believe not, sir. I am given to understand that they thought I was dead."

"But you weren't."

"No, sir."

"No, evidently. Mr. Scroby met his ancestors at a séance."

"Indeed, sir?" said Wilkins. He transferred his attention to Scroby, who described what had happened.

"I see, sir. Some sort of communication is to be expected before the gentlemen actually appear."

"If they were to walk in," said Scroby, "what would you do, Wilkins?"

"Do, sir? I hope I should conduct myself towards them exactly as in the case of any other visitor. It would not be my place to differentiate in any way between your visitors, sir. If they required any service of any kind, I should expect to supply it, sir, if obtainable."

"Obtainable?"

"I have no experience, sir, of what long-deceased ancestors are likely to require, if anything. Such experience as I have had of psychic phenomena has provided me with no data upon the point, sir."

"Wilkins," said Hawkes, "are you trying to tell us that you have seen a ghost?"

"Oh yes, sir, several times. When I was with Lord Welter, sir, his lordship's ancestor used to descend the great staircase with his head under his arm, sir. It was said that his previous lordship was beheaded in the reign of Henry VIII, sir. Some trouble with the lady Anne Boleyn, I was given to understand. Exchanging badinage, if I may so put it."

"A darned touchy gentleman, Henry VIII, by all accounts," said Hawkes.

"So it is said, sir. When I first went into service with the Dowager

Duchess of Grantham, sir, as a lad, there was a little girl in a blue frock as used to play with a ball in the long gallery, but I understood as nothing was known about her antecedents, sir."

"I see," said Scroby. "So you will find nothing incredible in the visible appearance of ancestors?"

"Nothing at all, sir. On the contrary, all the best families have them. They add a definite *cachet,* if I may be allowed to say so, sir. Will there be anything more, sir, at the moment?"

The following morning Scroby was awakened at half-past eight by his manservant coming in with the breakfast tray. Wilkins set down the tray on the bedside table, drew up the blinds, and returned to ask if he should pour out the coffee.

"What? Oh yes, please. Morning, Wilkins. What sort of a day is it?"

"A beautiful morning, sir, the sun is quite brilliant."

"Then fling the windows open wide, let in the morning air. I say, is that Tennyson or somebody, or did I compose it myself?"

"I cannot at the moment recall a context to the lines you have just recited, sir. It is conceivable, if I may say so, that the combination of a good night's rest, a quiet conscience, perfect health, and a first morning in Paris may conduce to the inadvertent production of poetry, sir."

"Oh," said Scroby, between gulps of coffee, "do you think so?"

"I should regard it as possible, sir. Excuse me, sir, there is a telegram."

Scroby put his cup down and turned pale.

"Wilkins, it isn't—it can't be—surely not from—from my aunt? Miss Scroby? Oh no, Wilkins."

"In view of the fact, sir, that Miss Scroby had no idea where we were going and has had less than twenty-four hours in which to track us down, I should regard it as remarkably unlikely, sir."

"Thank you, Wilkins. "

"Not at all, sir."

"But who can have sent it? Only Hawkes knows that I am here and he wouldn't send a telegram. He'd ring up."

"Yes, sir."

"I can't imagine whom it can be from," said Scroby, still stalling.

"If I might suggest, sir, a removal of the covering envelope and a perusal of the contents—"

"Yes, I know. Look, Wilkins, you open it. Then, if it is from Miss Scroby, I can truthfully maintain that I never saw it."

"Very good, sir." Wilkins opened the envelope and unfolded the sheet.

"It is signed 'Latimer,' sir."

"Latimer?"

" 'James and Charles Latimer,' sir. The message runs: 'Come at once to St. Denis-sur-Aisne, urgent.' "

Scroby seized his coffee cup, drained the contents too fast, and choked badly. When the consequent flurry had died away he lay back upon his pillows and said: "But that's impossible," in a weak voice.

"Indeed, sir?"

"Yes. James and Charles Latimer are the ancestors of whom I spoke to you last night. You remember."

"Very clearly, sir, but if my memory serves me, you did not mention their names."

"Oh, didn't I? Well, that's what they are, or were. Still are, I suppose. Do people keep their own names in the Hereafter, Wilkins, do you think?"

"I regret, sir, that I cannot call to mind any data upon which to form an opinion, though some means of verbal identification would seem to be convenient even in a state of perpetual bliss, sir."

"I daresay you're right."

"We must, in the words of a well-known politician, 'wait and see,' sir."

Scroby said rather wildly: "Perhaps James and Charles Latimer will tell us. Where was that telegram sent from?"

"From St. Denis-sur-Aisne, sir."

"Wilkins, this is ridiculous. Ghosts don't send telegrams."

Wilkins looked down at the carpet for a moment and then at Scroby.

"Excuse me, sir—"

"Well?"

"I seem to remember, sir, upon one occasion when Miss Scroby took tea with you that she referred in my hearing to some relatives named Latimer, sir. Americans, if my memory is not at fault, sir."

"You are quite right, she did. Second or third cousins of mine, from Richmond, Virginia. When I was over there as a kid, I met them, but I can't remember much about them now and I shouldn't know them if I met them face to face. Always playing practical jokes on people. I thought them great fun, but my aunt didn't approve at all."

"No, sir. I seem to recall that Miss Scroby's comments, on the occasion to which I refer, were markedly censorious, sir."

"She thought they had a bad influence over me. But, Wilkins, why did you— Wilkins! Do you mean—"

Wilkins permitted his features what was practically an indulgent smile.

"Practical joking, sir?"

"By gosh," said Scroby, sitting up so suddenly that Wilkins had to make a slip fielder's dive to preserve the breakfast tray, "by heavens, you've got it! They know the story, they know I'm here— How do they know I'm here?"

"I imagine, sir, that they must have been in the entrance hall of this hotel when we arrived and heard Mr. Hawkes announce your name, sir, and on hearing it they recognized—"

"That's right, that's right! And they heard Hawkes say that he'd come back to take me to that séance."

"I cannot recall, sir, hearing Mr. Hawkes state that the entertainment he proposed for you was a séance."

"Quite right, he didn't. He only told me as we went along. Never mind, they found out somehow. They bribed the woman who ran the show, the—"

"Medium, sir?"

"—the medium to give that message. And Hawkes must be in the joke, too, since he took me to the séance. Now they're at St. Denis-sur-Aisne, wherever that is, and want me to go and meet them. Jolly good show. We'll go, Wilkins, today."

"Yes, sir."

"Where is the place, do you know at all? Have we got any maps? I wonder how far it is."

"I have never visited the place in question, sir, but if it is on the Aisne it will not be more than, say, a hundred miles or thereabouts, sir."

"Splendid. We were going to hire a car for you to drive. Go out at once, Wilkins, and see what you can get hold of while I'm getting dressed."

"Very good, sir."

"Oh, and get some road maps of France."

"Yes, sir. A substantial deposit upon the car will, I believe, be required to be paid."

"You find a car," said Scroby, with his mouth full of bacon and egg, "and I'll come and settle up for it. It's a good thing I'm an American citizen; the English travel allowance wouldn't stand up to this sort of thing. Is there anything else to settle before you start, Wilkins?"

"Have you any preferences in regard to the car, sir?"

"I leave the choice of car entirely to your discretion, Wilkins, with the utmost confidence. Not too enormous, of course. Reasonable in size; but for the rest, you're going to drive it."

"Very good, sir. Thank you, sir."

"On your way, Wilkins."

"Immediately, sir."

On the previous evening, the village of St. Denis-sur-Aisne drowsed in its wonted peace. One by one the lights went out in the houses on either side of the long street; only at the Hôtel du Commerce a few windows were still lighted in case the 11:45 P.M. train from Paris should bring a visitor desiring accommodation; the post office also showed a light at a side window where Mlle. Grober, the postmaster's daughter, sat within earshot of the telephone switchboard and kept some soup warm at the side of the stove in case her father should come in chilly and hungry from the Paris train. All five plate-glass windows of Vigneron's departmental store were in darkness, and so were those of the flat above, where M. Vigneron lived with a useful sister. André's garage was dark and silent, for André had gone home to bed. The only other lighted window in the village was at the police station, and that one was unnoticeable except upon the very darkest nights, for it had an indigo-blue blind drawn down over it. Inside the police station, Sergeant Boulestier sat at his desk with a glass of wine at his elbow, finishing a report and filling up time till Constable Vautout should come in at the end of his patrol and report that all was quiet in St. Denis-sur-Aisne, and all well. There was no reason why Boulestier should not simply go to bed and leave the utterly reliable Vautout to lock up; the fact was that Boulestier was a slave to habit; for the thirty-four years he had been Constable there he had, so to speak, seen the village in bed and asleep before retiring himself, and he would have felt uncomfortable if he had changed his custom. Besides, it impressed his wife.

As the hands of the clock crept on to a quarter past eleven, the door opened and Vautout came in.

"All quiet at the north end of the village, *mon Sergent.* Monsieur le Docteur has been called out to a confinement at Les Deux Chênes farm. The Widow Maillot has found her dog which was lost."

Boulestier grunted and Vautout shifted his feet.

"Otherwise," he said slowly, "everything seems quiet enough."

Boulestier took off his steel-framed spectacles and turned his ruminative gaze upon his Constable.

" 'Seems?' What do you mean, 'seems'?"

"I do not know, *mon Sergent.* That is—I do not know."

"Have you, then, seen anything to make you uneasy?"

"Nothing, *mon Sergent.* Everything appears to be normal."

"Are there people about?"

"No, *mon Sergent.* Since Monsieur le Docteur drove out and spoke to me in passing, I have seen and heard no one."

"Oh. Not even the daughter of the postmaster at her gate?"

Vautout looked down and blushed, for he was an ingenuous young man.

"Not even Mademoiselle Grober. No, it is just a—a sort of feeling. As though people were looking at me, but there is no one about, *mon Sergent.* One shivers, without cause. A tendency to look behind one—" He stopped, suddenly afraid of having earned a reprimand for foolishness.

But Sergeant Boulestier's heavy face expressed nothing but its usual ox-like patience, and at that moment the telephone rang upon the desk. The Sergeant lifted the receiver.

"St. Denis police station . . . . Indeed. What sort of noises? . . . Indeed . . . indeed. At once, mademoiselle." He replaced the receiver and looked across at Vautout with an expression of mild amusement.

"It is Mademoiselle Grober, at the post office. She says there are unaccountable noises in the office although, when she went in, there was nothing. She is alone in the house; her father returns on the Paris train tonight. She is alarmed." Boulestier's impassive face broke into a slow grin. "You have twenty minutes to investigate this complaint, Vautout; you will resume your patrol when the Paris train is due. Then report to me."

"Very good, *mon Sergent,*" said Vautout, and bolted out of the room.

The smile left Boulestier's face and a look of interest replaced it. "Odd," he murmured, "odd. A quiet, well-conducted young woman, she would hardly— Those quiet ones, you never know. I ought to have gone myself, should I? But I was courting, once. I will wait a little."

Vautout dashed up to the post office and found Mlle. Grober waiting at the side door.

"What is it, Mademoiselle Germaine? Have you—"

She drew him inside and closed the door, which led to the Grober sitting room at the back of the post office itself. There was a curtained archway from the sitting room to a small lobby where the telephone switchboard was installed; one passed through this lobby to the post office at the front of the house. Vautout looked at the girl, who was white and shivering, and took her hand respectfully.

"Tell me—"

She led him into the telephone lobby; the door admitting to the post office was shut and locked and there was no light showing through the glass panel.

"Listen," she whispered, and Vautout cocked his head.

"People moving," he murmured.

"In the dark?" she said, and moved closer to him.

"I shall go in," he said. "Is the door locked?"

"But I have been in," she said, "and there is no one there."

"Give me the key," he said, and she put it into his hand. He opened the door, switched on the light, and went in; the Grober cat, which had been fidgeting at the door, slipped between his legs and rushed in before him.

There was no one there. Vautout walked into the middle of the office and looked keenly about him while the girl watched him from the doorway; suddenly, as he stood there, he shivered violently and she saw it.

"What is it, Etienne?"

"Nothing." Vautout walked all around the office, examining the door fastenings, looking in every corner and under the counters; there was nothing there except the cat, which appeared to be playing some kind of charade with itself, tail erect and purring loudly.

Vautout came back to the girl. "There is nothing there. Where were you when you heard the noise?"

"Sitting at the switchboard here, with my knitting. There have been some calls put through tonight; there is a new baby at Les Deux Chênes, a son, they have been telling her people; some people at the Hôtel du Commerce have had calls, so I sat there—Look at that cat! Joyeuse! Joyeuse! Come out."

But the cat took no notice and went on performing figures of eight in the middle of the floor.

"Shut the door," said Germaine Grober, "she will drive me silly doing that."

Vautout shut the door between them and the office but left the light on; they stood close together and talked in anxious whispers.

"It is mice," said Vautout. "Joyeuse smells mice."

"There have been no mice here since they changed the gum on the stamps," she said. "Besides, everything is locked up. Besides, that is not how cats behave when they smell mice. She has been strange for the past half hour, patting at the door and mewing to get in. Always, when I am on duty at the telephone, she sleeps on her cushion beside me there, you know. Tonight, she was there and suddenly she woke up and ran to the door as you saw. Etienne, what is it, all this?"

Vautout found that he was holding both her hands in his. He could not remember how it had happened, but there it was, and very agreeable, too. He had been wishing to hold them for long enough. He looked down at the troubled face so near his own.

"Mon adorée, mon adorée—"

And at precisely that moment someone in the office dropped some coins on the counter. Germaine uttered what can only be described as a yelp of terror and the next moment was in his arms and clinging to him. Her hair tickled his chin and Vautout was surprised to find that the mysterious noises in the office were far less important than the feel of a girl's soft hair under his chin. Also, he was no longer nervous. Whatever it was in the office could wait his convenience.

"Adorable Germaine, ma petite—"

After a brief but satisfactory interlude she pushed him gently but firmly away and pointed the finger of duty at the post office door. Vautout drew a long breath, straightened his shoulders, opened the door, and strode in. Joyeuse was standing near the door going through the motions of a cat being stroked, ducking her head, curtseying and coming up again, purring aloud. One could almost see the hand stroking steadily from head to tail. Suddenly she straightened up, ran to the outer door, and stared at it.

Germaine came in and said sharply: "There is a telegram on the counter. And the money to pay for it."

"It was not there before," said Vautout. "When I came in before, there was nothing on the counter. I am trained to observe things, and the counter was bare."

Germaine automatically, as one in a dream, counted the words in the telegram and the money on the counter.

"The sum is correct," she said in a dazed voice.

"Who sent it—what is the signature?"

She looked at him reproachfully. "You are not thinking what you say; you know very well it is against the rules to communicate the contents of a telegram to any unauthorized person. Are you authorized for this purpose, Etienne?"

"No. Only for the purpose of protecting you."

"Then I cannot help it if you hear me sending it, can I?" she said, and dimpled at him.

"My sweet! But are you—will you send it?"

"But, certainly. It is properly made out and paid for; it is my duty to send it. Come, let us lock this door again and go in the other room. Will you put the light out here?"

She paused abruptly in the lobby by the telephone switchboard. "Look!"

The cat Joyeuse was peacefully curled up on her cushion, sound asleep.

"The ways of cats," said Vautout, "are beyond our understanding. Monsieur Vigneron's cat Tigre also, I have seen him playing the oddest games by himself. One would say, playacting."

"One moment," she said, "while I send this off. Do not leave me alone, Etienne."

"Never again, if I could help it—"

"You are disordering my hair—just a moment, while I send this off—"

Eventually it was sent, to an audience of Vautout and the cat Joyeuse. "Come at once," said the telegram, "to St. Denis-sur-Aisne, urgent," and it was signed "James and Charles Latimer."

"No one of that name," said Germaine, "lives in our village."

"No," said Vautout, "although the name suggests something to me. But at the moment I have something better to think about. Come in by the fire, Germaine. Oh, *mon Dieu!* Look at the clock! It is the Paris train which is due; I must go. Boulestier told me to go back upon patrol at this time."

"Do not leave me until Papa comes—I am still nervous—you cannot be so unkind."

"My duty," said Vautout desperately, and took up his cap. "Boulestier will say—"

"I will ring him up," she said, and returned to the telephone to explain that the Constable's continued protection was advisable until M. Grober returned. Vautout heard indistinguishable growls from the receiver as Boulestier answered, and Germaine uttered a shocked squeal of protest and hung up the receiver with a bang.

"What did he say?"

"That you can stay," she said, but her cheeks were scarlet.

"What else?"

"I'll never tell you, never—never!"

CHAPTER V
The Latimers

THE HIRED Citroën, with Wilkins driving and Scroby sitting beside him, came slowly up the single long street of St. Denis just before noon.

"I don't," said Scroby, looking carefully at such of the inhabitants as were on view in the dinner hour, "see anyone who looks in the least like an American cousin. The people in this place appear to me to be even more French than usual."

"If I may say so without presumption, the observation is both penetrating and accurate, sir. The remoter the village, the less accessible to— er—foreign influences, sir."

"Oh—ah. Yes, I suppose so. Drive on through the village and then turn and come back, Wilkins. Probably my cousins are having lunch somewhere, but I've no idea where to look for them or even what they look like if I do see them. This seems to be the end, Wilkins."

"Yes, sir. I will back into this gateway and turn."

"Wilkins. I have had an idea. Yes, turn round, I haven't changed my mind. We will go to the post office, show them this telegram, and ask for a description of the people who sent it, what?"

"An inspiration, sir."

"Thank you, Wilkins."

"Not at all, sir."

They drove back to the post office. Scroby leapt out of the car and dashed in, arranging phrases in his mind as he went. A dancing bell jangled above his head as he opened the door and an elderly man came from somewhere behind the counter, wiping his mouth on a large white napkin.

"*Monsieur désire?*"

"Er—*bonjour.*"

"*Bonjour, monsieur,*" said the postmaster, raising his eyebrows.

"Er—do you speak English? I mean, *parlez-vous anglais?*"

"*Mais non, monsieur. Je regrette.*"

"So do I, by gosh. Never mind, I'll do my best." Scroby frowned, gathered his wits, and plunged. Could Monsieur say who sent this telegram? (Produced.)

M. Grober, speaking slowly and using the simplest words:

"*Mais non. Un moment. J'appelle ma fille.*"

He left the room and Scroby translated aloud. " 'But no. One moment. I call my daughter.' This is all right, I only want practice."

Grober returned, followed by a blue-eyed fair girl with a businesslike expression. Grober showed her the telegram and said that Monsieur wanted to know who had sent it. Germaine looked at it, turned pale, leaned against the counter and said she didn't know.

"Pardon?" said Scroby.

"*Elle ne sait pas*," said Grober, and picked up the telegram.

"*Je ne sais pas, monsieur*," said the girl, shaking her head.

"But," said Scroby, "I mean, *mais, qui était* here *quand la télégramme fut—fut* brought in? *Si ce* wasn't you, *qui c'était?*"

Grober dived through the door behind him and came back with the original telegraph form. He showed it to his daughter, pointing out, in a flood of his native tongue, that her initials as sender were upon it. She nodded and agreed that she had sent it, but—Grober then noticed the time of dispatch which Germaine had entered correctly as 23 hours 38 minutes and wanted to know why she had kept it hanging about for three hours after the office closed. Germaine said that it hadn't been brought in until late and she had dispatched it within ten minutes. Grober demanded why the office had been still open at that hour; he supposed she had been wasting her time talking to that oaf of a constable who had the insolence to be still here when he, Grober, returned. Germaine flared up at this and told Grober the office was haunted and she wouldn't stay there another day. She described what had happened in a voice rising steadily against Grober's loud and acid comments until they were both talking at once in a language of which poor Scroby only recognized three words, *la chatte Joyeuse* several times repeated, though what a joyous female cat had to do with it was quite beyond him.

"I don't understand French after all," he said unhappily, and went to the door to beckon Wilkins, who came running.

"I can't understand one word they say, Wilkins."

Wilkins bent an ear to the argument still in progress behind the counter, shook his head, marched up to the grille and rapped sharply with the edge of a coin. He had been in the Army in the Second World War and the British Tommy is not fazed by foreign tongues. He simply utters words which sound like something and the foreigner somehow understands. No one has ever explained this phenomenon. When Wilkins intervened, Grober and his daughter stopped as though someone had turned their taps off.

Wilkins spoke, with brief pauses for thought they answered, and some half-dozen sentences were exchanged. Wilkins ended with "Mercy bokoo," and turned to Scroby.

"They didn't see who brought the wire in, sir."

"Oh," said Scroby, pained and annoyed, "then why didn't they simply say so?"

"I could not take it upon myself to say, sir. These foreigners do tend to over-dramatization, sir."

Scroby drifted dispiritedly out, followed by Wilkins.

"But what were they arguing about?"

"The first I heard, sir, was the young person saying that she was going to marry a policeman, sir."

"But what the hell's that got to do with my telegram?"

"I could not venture a guess, sir."

"Gaga," said Scroby. "Let's go to the hotel. The Latimers might be there, and anyway, I want my lunch."

Scroby entered the dining room of the Hôtel du Commerce and was conducted to a small table near the window; Wilkins, who had somehow detached himself on entering the hotel, sat at the far end near the serving-hatch. Since Scroby had nothing to do but order from an attentive waiter recognizable items from the menu, he managed very well and was quite pleased with himself until he caught a glimpse, between potted palms, of Wilkins with a couple of serving maids leaning upon his table. They were conversing in a most animated manner and their evident amusement was only restrained by respect for the company.

Scroby sighed and finished his soup.

Presently a stout and dignified figure entered the room and stopped in the doorway to look magisterially about him; the serving wenches fled. The man advanced into the room and passed from table to table with a few smiling words at each one and an eagle eye for any deficiency.

"The proprietor," said Scroby. "Now for it."

When the proprietor reached Scroby's table he stopped, bowed, and said that he hoped everything was satisfactory. Scroby nodded and thanked him and then asked in well-rehearsed phrases whether any gentlemen named Latimer were at the hotel.

The proprietor's face lit up. Ah! He had the honor to address Monsieur Scroby?

Scroby said: *"Mais oui. Mon nom est Scroby."*

The proprietor had had English visitors before and had evolved a formula for mutual comprehension. One—or two—words at a time and give them time to sink.

"*J'ai—une lettre—pour Monsieur. Comprenez?*"

Scroby nodded eagerly; the innkeeper said, "*Un moment;*" and scurried away. Scroby relaxed; this was French as it should be offered. There was a letter, good.

The man came back with a letter on a salver and stood back while Scroby opened it. It was written in a slanting, pointed handwriting which looked oddly old-fashioned, and ran:

> *Dear Cousin Richard Scroby,*
>
> *We are so sorry that we are not able to meet you here but we will join you on the road to Paris. Would you be so obliging as to collect our valises from the proprietor here who has been housing them for us? He has our authority to hand them to you. We must apologize for burdening you with them, pray forgive the imposition.*
>
> *Anticipating with keen pleasure our early meeting, we remain,*
>
> *Your affectionate cousins,*
> *James Latimer,*
> *Charles Latimer.*

> *P.S. Do not forget the baggage.*

Scroby read it twice and then looked round; the proprietor hurried forward. "You will take the two cases, monsieur?"

Scroby said rather uncertainly that he would and managed to ask where his cousins were.

"I have not seen them, monsieur, not since last year in September."

"Oh! They were here then?"

But yes, certainly. But not today. That is to say, the innkeeper had not seen them today. A note was left. A note to the innkeeper. It said the suitcases—were to be given—to Monsieur Scroby—when he should come. Understood?

Scroby nodded and the proprietor beamed upon him.

"Monsieur stays here? A night? A few days?"

Scroby said no, he was returning to Paris, at once. It was necessary.

The proprietor said that he was desolated but Monsieur must return. To St. Denis, come again, yes?

Scroby smiled and agreed and the proprietor made way for a waiter with a dish of which the contents were obscure but delectable.

"They can cook here," said Scroby, and abandoned the thought of his mysterious cousins for the pleasures of the table.

When he was ready to go, two good-looking suitcases were brought out from the proprietor's office and ceremoniously placed in the boot of the Citroën. There was a stout and busy woman, whom Scroby correctly placed as the proprietor's wife, who was talking in the hall when the cases were borne past her. She looked at them with an odd expression which Scroby could not define and then most interestedly at him, a long look which was nearly a stare.

"My wife," said the proprietor to Scroby, and then to her: "This is the Monsieur Scroby who is related to the Messieurs Latimer."

Scroby said: "Oh—how d'you do," the woman said: *"Enchantée, monsieur,"* but somehow did not look it, Scroby got into the car, the proprietor waved farewell, and Wilkins drove away.

"That is my cousins' luggage in the back," said Scroby. "They wanted me to take it."

"Indeed, sir."

"They are joining us," said Scroby in an offhand voice, "somewhere on the road to Paris."

"Very good, sir."

There was a short silence.

"But they didn't say where."

Wilkins opened his mouth to speak, shut it again, and then said that the omission to particularize a meeting place might prove to be frustrating, sir. He asked if Scroby wished to turn back and ask them.

"They weren't there," said Scroby. "They left a note."

"In that case, sir," said Wilkins, and paused.

"Precisely," said Scroby. "Well, it's been a pleasant drive and they know my address in Paris."

"Yes, sir," said Wilkins, and drove on.

He was an excellent driver; Scroby, who drove a car himself at home in England, never had a moment's qualms with Wilkins at the wheel. It was all the more shocking, therefore, when about five miles further on, Wilkins suddenly swerved half across the road and missed by the narrowest of margins a heavy lorry which was pounding along towards them.

"Look out, Wilkins! You nearly hit him!"

"Yes, sir," said Wilkins in a shaking voice. "I apologize, sir, I do indeed."

Scroby looked at him and noticed that he was biting his lip, his face was white, and little beads of perspiration were gathering on his temples.

"What's the matter? Aren't you well?"

"I felt a little shaken for the moment, sir. No doubt it will soon pass."

"Stop at this café here," said Scroby, with concern in his voice. "Pull in off the road. What you want is a nip of brandy. What happened, did you feel giddy?"

Wilkins did not answer. He slowed down, turned the car off the road and upon the car-park of a roadside café, and stopped. He switched off the engine, pulled the handbrake on, and took out his handkerchief to wipe his face. Scroby leapt out of his side of the car and ran round the bonnet, but by the time he reached Wilkins' door the manservant was out of the car.

"Come along," said Scroby kindly. "We'll sit at one of those little tables outside and get the waiter to bring us something to drink. It is pleasant to be out in the air."

"Thank you, sir. Excuse me, sir. Will the two gentlemen in the back seat be taking a little refreshment?"

Scroby was seriously alarmed. The imperturbable Wilkins whom nothing ever disturbed was not only ill but plainly delirious.

"What d'you mean? The car's empty."

"It was, sir, when we left St. Denis. Allow me," said Wilkins. He stepped back, opened the rear door of the car, and held it for two men to alight. The first was a big fair man with a high color and blue-gray eyes; the second was a couple of inches taller but lean in build and walked like a horseman; he was tanned with the sun and had dark eyes, straight black hair, and a wide mouth which turned up at the corners. The first man looked anxiously apologetic, the second amusedly rueful.

"It was, sir, when I looked in the driving-mirror and saw the gentlemen just behind, sir, that I swerved towards the lorry, sir," said Wilkins in tones which were still agitated and a little pained. Scroby was so utterly taken aback that he could not speak at all. The fair man came up to him and took his hand in a warm firm grasp.

"Cousin Richard Scroby, this is indeed a pleasure and I am delighted to make your acquaintance. I am James Latimer of Oakwood Hall, Didsbury, and this is my cousin and yours, Charles Latimer of Shandon, Virginia."

Charles came up to shake hands, and his grip was as firm and friendly as the other's.

"Cousin Richard, this surely is a pleasure, yes, sir. Though I fear that our unconventional arrival discomposed your manservant. We do apologize," said Charles, turning his brilliant eyes and wide smile upon Wilkins. "My good man, I hope that you are now recovered."

"Thank you, sir," said Wilkins noncommittally. He shut the car door, sidled round the group, and went on towards the café.

"Yes, indeed," said James. "We are prodigious sorry to have startled your man so severely. We wondered whether we ought to attract your attention by speaking to you, but while we yet hesitated, he looked up and saw us."

"Y-yes," stammered Scroby. "I—that is—I thought he was taken ill— how d'you do?" He found himself feverishly shaking hands with both of them all over again. "I didn't expect quite that. Silly of me." He laughed nervously. "Let's go and all have a drink together, shall we? I must admit you startled me. Can't think why I didn't see you get in at St. Denis." He turned to lead the way towards the café, which had a small lawn in front with little round tables having chairs set about them. "It just shows," said Scroby, rapidly recovering himself, "how unobservant one can be. I thought there was no one in the back of the car so I never looked." As they walked on, a front window of the café came in line with some window at the back; silhouetted against this Scroby recognized the profile of Wilkins with a glass to its lips. The profile tilted upwards, the glass went with it until it passed the horizontal, paused, and was quickly taken away as the changing line of sight moved the scene from view. The café proprietor came out to take their orders; the Latimers asked if he had a passable claret and were offered a Côte du Rhône and Scroby applauded their choice. The man went away and the cousins sat down and looked at each other.

"How delightful all this is," said Charles. "The bright sunlight, the green grass and the gay flowerbeds with which this man has decorated his premises. Cousin Richard, it is a childish taste, but I do love striped umbrellas," and he looked up at the red and yellow one over their table.

"Jolly, aren't they?" agreed Scroby. "What I like even better are strings of colored electric lights, and if there is a crowd present when they are switched on, all the people say 'A—a—ah' together."

"The simplest pleasures," said James Latimer, "are as a rule the most enchanting. Perhaps they reawaken that sense of wonder which recalls the child which once we were."

The man from the café came out with a tray of glasses and saved Scroby from having to find an answer.

"My man," said Scroby to the proprietor, "is he all right? He was not very well."

The man looked blank and Charles laughed and translated. Apparently Wilkins had had a little glass for his stomach and was now much restored. Scroby blushed hotly.

"It's terribly stupid," he said, "but, do you know, I keep on forgetting these people don't understand English. I'm not at all good at French and what one learned at school may help one to speak but it's pretty hopeless when they answer back. I got in an awful tangle at the post office at St. Denis this morning. I didn't know what you looked like—I'm ashamed to say I don't remember you a bit—so I went in with the telegram to ask what you were like, but it didn't work."

"But, my dear boy," said James, "how could you possibly remember us when you have never seen us before?"

"But," said Scroby, "you are two of my American cousins, aren't you? I remember when I was a small boy and was taken to see my grand-mother Latimer at Richmond, Virginia, you were staying there too. There were three of you, weren't there? It was you, wasn't it?" He looked from one to the other. "I suppose you are two whom I didn't meet, but in that case how did you recognize me? Oh, I am a fool. Of course, Hawkes told you I was coming to Paris." He smiled upon them as one who has solved a problem. "Good fellow, Hawkes, isn't he? We were at school together. Is that wine all right?"

"A very pleasant wine indeed, if a little immature," said James.

"I am sure, Cousin," said Charles, "that your friend Hawkes is a most charming fellow, yes, sir, and we look forward with pleasure to making his acquaintance. But, up to now, we have never met him."

"He's the man who took me to the séance, you know," said Scroby, anxious that there should be no misunderstanding. "Tall thin chap with a long nose. He told me that he was going to the séance to try to find out whether the medium is genuine or a fraud, and wanted me to come too just for fun. That's what he said: of course, I realize now that it was a put-up job to get me there so that the medium could hand me out your mes-sage. Jolly good show. I admit quite frankly that I was completely foxed last night; it wasn't till this morning that it dawned on me how it was worked."

The Latimers looked at each other and Charles broke into a laugh. "My stars," he said. "Cousin Richard, you certainly are the possessor of a penetrating and ingenious mind, yes, sir. I hand it to you, Cousin Richard Scroby." He laughed again with such genuine amusement that Scroby had to laugh with him. "Gentlemen, hush! Almost you convince me that that is how it was. How say you, Cousin James?"

Scroby, who had spent most of his life being persuaded by his aunt that he was practically dim-witted, blushed with pleasure. James looked at him with kindness but also with a certain austerity which reminded him of being at school. Your algebra paper, Scroby, is doubtless well intentioned, but—

"Ingenious indeed, but quite mistaken," said James. "My dear Richard, the medium was not fraudulent, far from it, and she transmitted our message in a most praiseworthy manner, apart from a certain blundering over our names. We were informed that you were at the séance and we were permitted to send you a message because, it seems, you are in some sort of difficulty, or even danger, and will need our services."

Scroby finished his wine, set down the glass carefully, leaned back in his chair, and looked from one to the other. Of course the whole thing was a hoax, but they had taken an immense amount of trouble to arrange this affair, it would be almost ungrateful to call their bluff too soon. Let them carry on as long as they liked; they were nice fellows and it was all rather fun.

"It is evident," continued James, "that you do not yet understand who and what we are, but we have told you twice; at the séance and again here. I am James Latimer and this is Charles and we were shot by the Prussians in 1870."

"You must surely have heard the story, Cousin," said Charles. "We are the two who were missing."

Scroby nodded and managed to look convincingly astonished.

"You are naturally surprised, Richard," said James. "Believe me, there is no cause for perturbation. These things are as they are permitted to be and not otherwise."

"Are you trying in real earnest to tell me that you two are ghosts?" asked Scroby innocently.

"Certainly," said Charles cheerfully. "That is what we are when we are back in this material world. We could so easily prove it, too, but that we are within full view of several persons of both sexes and it is discourteous and unkind to frighten people who have done nothing to deserve it."

"Such a practice," said James severely, "would be frowned upon, and rightly. We are permitted to return to help people, not to play the pretentious bugaboo of a fireside story."

"But you are completely solid," objected Scroby. "Warm and tangible and—and ordinary, if you know what I mean."

"Cousin Richard, sir," said Charles, "you would not have us glide about in grave-clothes, pale green and faintly phosphorescent, rattling chains and mooing like a sick cow?"

Wilkins came from the café, drawing on his gloves, and passed them on his way to the car.

"Wilkins," said Scroby, "these gentlemen say they are ghosts. Can you believe it? I mean, they look so normal, don't they, Wilkins?"

"If I may say so, gentlemen," said Wilkins with a polite bow to the Latimers, "my first glimpse of you in the driving-mirror occurred at what might be called the semisolid stage of your arrival, gentlemen. It was the rapid evolution from transparency to solidity, if I may so put it, which riveted my attention to the point where I narrowly missed the oncoming vehicle."

"That was all provided for, Wilkins," said Charles. "Had you been completely nonplussed, I should have leapt to the rescue in good time."

"Thank you, sir," said Wilkins. "May I enquire, sir, whether, if at any time in the future I should chance upon you in an intermediate stage, would it be your wish that I should avert my eyes?"

"As if you had come upon us changing our pants?" laughed Charles. "It does not matter, Wilkins, at all."

"Thank you, sir," said Wilkins.

Scroby was glad of an opportunity to laugh with Charles, for he found the situation most entertaining. His American cousins had a reputation for practical joking, and if these two were fair samples of the family, the reputation was well deserved. A pair of star turns, in his opinion; it would be interesting to see how long they would keep it up.

As for what Wilkins thought he saw, that was nonsense.

He probably saw them in the act of getting up from the floor of the car and imagined the rest. Scroby remembered "the previous Lord Welter" with his head under his arm. Wilkins was definitely ghost-minded.

CHAPTER VI
Ulysses

WILKINS having completely recovered, they returned to the car and drove on towards Paris with the Latimers together in the rear seat and Scroby sitting slowed round in front, talking to them.

"The landlord of the Hôtel du Commerce," said Scroby, "told me that you were there last year. I suppose you often—er—come out, do you?"

"Under certain circumstances," said James, "we are permitted to return; that is, if there is some problem to be solved or some difficulty to be overcome in connection with our own family, and provided also that someone of our own blood comes to St. Denis-sur-Aisne to give us the strength to materialize."

"That, Cousin Richard," said Charles, "is why we had to ask you to come in person to St. Denis. Tell me, do you know your cousins Jeremy and Sally Latimer?"

"Only by name, I've never met them. Oh yes, by the way, aren't they the cousins who somehow found out where—er—James and Charles Latimer were and had them properly buried in a churchyard somewhere? I remember now, Aunt Angela heard about it from someone and told me. Wasn't there a pet monkey in the story somewhere?"

"There is," said Charles. "He bit the Prussian officer, so the Sergeant shot him."

Scroby grinned appreciatively. It was just that sort of colorful detail which made a story convincing.

"But your clothes," he said, looking them over, "are not of 1870, are they? They look practically new and quite modern."

"Oh, these are not the clothes we died in," said James. "We found that if we walked about in our own dress we attracted too much attention. We were actually pointed at, Cousin, by those of the lower sort, a thing intolerable to any gentleman."

"They thought," said Charles with a bubble of laughter, "that we were advertising a performance of living pictures called, I believe, *Gone with the Wind*. Cousin, I opine they expected us to beat a drum and cry 'Walk up! Walk up!' We certainly caused comment, yes, sir."

"It was most distasteful," said James, "as you may imagine. So we took steps to obtain these suits which, if not of a cut and material comparable with yours, are yet passable in France. But we have talked enough about ourselves, Cousin Richard, indeed, too much. Tell us about yourself now; you are of the American branch and so most nearly connected with Charles, here, but you do not speak like an American."

"I was taken to England when I was four," explained Scroby, "and I have lived there ever since, that's why. You heard about my parents being killed in a road accident, did you?"

"We did, indeed," said Charles sympathetically.

"It was a tragedy for you," said James in his deepest chest-voice, "to be deprived of the tender care of both parents at so early an age."

"I can't remember them," said Scroby hastily. "My father's sister Angela took charge of me and we went to live in England."

"I assume," said James, "that your aunt Angela Scroby had the good taste to marry an Englishman."

"Oh no. That was why we came to England, you see."

"I would say," said Charles with a laugh, "that that is what we were taught at school to call a *non sequitur.* Yes, sir."

"Pray continue," said James. "Your good aunt came to England because she did not marry an Englishman—"

"It does sound a bit mad, put like that. Aunt Angela met an English Army officer during the First World War; he went over to the States on some training scheme and they got engaged. But he came back over here and was killed, and ever since she has thought that everything English is marvelous. If they'd married, she would have been English, you see, so now she's as English as possible to—to sort of make up, I suppose. And of course she had no children of her own, so when she took charge of me I had to be brought over to England too. That's all."

"A romantic and touching story," said James. "We men should feel humbled in the presence of so lifelong a faith. Such a woman is an example to her sex."

Scroby thought of his aunt Angela and a variety of emotions seized upon him; Charles, who was watching his expressive face, looked faintly amused.

"Is your aunt with you in Paris?"

"Oh no," said Scroby, "no. She doesn't care much for traveling and I came over rather on the spur of the moment. But about you, do you generally leave a suitcase at the Hôtel du Commerce? Or is it sometimes at one place and sometimes at another? St. Denis-sur-Aisne is a nice little place, no doubt, but—"

"It is convenient to leave our things at that hotel," said James. "The landlord is honest and they are safe in his care, an important point, since we leave our money in them."

"I see," said Scroby.

"And as for it being at St. Denis," continued James, "it is true it is a dull little place, but we have no choice. You see, we are buried there."

That, Scroby thought, was extremely good; just so they would probably talk if they really were the men they claimed to be. For one dizzy moment he wondered whether they were, and then recovered himself. If he let himself be led into believing all that, the practical joke would succeed beyond hope. Ghosts, indeed! Drinking wine and smoking his cigarettes. He began to talk about Paris and it seemed that they knew the place well, even the Basilica du Sacré Coeur and the Eiffel Tower, neither of which was there in 1870. Scroby nearly told them to be more careful.

Wilkins drew up at the door of the Lune d'Italie and his passengers got out.

"Come up to my room," said Scroby. "Oh, there's your luggage in the back. Wilkins—"

But the hall porter was there and firmly took charge of the two cases. "The car, she can remain for the present," he said. "The gentlemen may wish to go out in her later, perhaps? Splendid. She will be quite safe there, it is not the day for the police to come."

"The police—" began Scroby.

"It is most strictly *défen*—I mean, forbidden to park cars on the other side of the road," explained the porter. "It makes that there is too little room enough for the traffic, you understand? So, the police. But they were here yesterday so they will not come today, eh? Splendid." He put down the luggage in a corner of the hall.

"But," said the law-abiding Scroby, "if it is forbidden—Wilkins! Have we anywhere to garage the car?"

"It is all arranged, sir. If the car is not required again tonight I am to telephone the garage and they will fetch it, sir."

"Oh. All right. Let's go up, shall we? It's only on the first floor." He led the way up the graceful winding stair with its wrought-iron balustrades and along the passage to his own room. Wilkins slipped past them to unlock the door.

"But this is delightful," said James. "A private sitting room. Most convenient."

"Charming," said Charles, and crossed the room to look out of the window. "What a press of traffic in this narrow street; it is one which has never been modernized. The good Baron Haussmann overlooked this one."

"Do sit down," said Scroby. "What will you have? Wilkins, what have we got in the cupboard?"

"Would the gentlemen care for sherry, sir? I also obtained what the salesman assured me was a good claret and there is brandy and some liqueurs. The port is not settled yet, sir."

"Quite a cellar," said Charles. "Cousin Richard, I opine that you are a man who knows how to live, yes, sir. May I have a glass of claret?"

"And for me also, since you are so hospitable," said James. "I always loved a good claret."

"And sherry for me, Wilkins," added Scroby. The Latimers sat down together upon the sofa between the windows and Scroby opposite to them. He offered cigarettes and asked where the Latimers were staying in Paris.

"That is," he went on, "if you require anywhere to stay, or do you just vanish when you want to go to bed?" Charles laughed aloud and even James smiled. "I seem to have dropped a brick," said Scroby as Wilkins came back with a tray. "You see, I don't really know—"

His voice died away because there was something on the sofa between Charles and James which had not been there before. It was rather indistinct although the light was good, but it was moving. It looked like an animal of some kind; it was a monkey, wearing a little red jacket and a tiny round hat to match. It was jumping up and down and becoming clearer every moment, though Scroby saw without believing that the back of the sofa was plainly visible through it.

At that moment Wilkins, who had had his eyes upon three full glasses, set the tray down carefully upon the table and looked up. An agonized cry was wrung from him.

"Cor blimey O'Reilly! *What's that?*"

"That," said Charles, turning to pick up the animal, "is my little monkey, Ulysses. You mentioned him yourself, Cousin Richard, did you not?"

"I know," said Scroby faintly, for his head was singing loudly and he felt as though his hands did not belong to him, "I know. He shot the Prussian officer."

He found himself leaning forward with his head between his knees and James' firm hand upon the back of his neck. The windows had been opened widely, and what in Paris passes for fresh air was blowing in upon his face. Scroby sat up and the singing in his head retreated to the distance; he blinked and saw the hand of Charles Latimer close under his nose offering a small glass of cognac to his lips. Scroby took it and drank and left off shivering.

"I'm most frightfully sorry," he began, "can't think what made me do that—"

"My dear boy," said James anxiously, "are you indeed covered? Come and rest upon the sofa. Charles, your arm. There. Do you still like the air upon your face?"

"I do feel all kinds of a fool," said Scroby, leaning back and looking from one to the other. "You must excuse me—where's the monkey?"

"I sent him away," said Charles, "since the sight of him discomposed you. Cousin, if you are naturally averse to monkeys you shall never see him again."

"It isn't that," said Scroby. "You see, I didn't—that is, I thought you were joking all the time. Aren't you? You can't really be ghosts, can you? Or are you? Surely not. I'd got it all worked out."

"But we told you," said James.

"I know you did, but I thought it was part of the act."

Charles laughed and James said that it was an excellent example of the manner in which a preconceived opinion will blind even men of education and intelligence to the value of plain evidential fact.

Scroby rubbed his eyes and Charles said: "Do you believe it now or shall we demonstrate in our own persons?"

"Not just at the moment, thanks," said Scroby rather too hastily, and then, with an awkward feeling of having been uncivil to guests, he added: "Let's have the monkey back, can we?"

Ulysses appeared upon the table, a small Capuchin monkey with soft brown hair all over his body and the typical "Capuchin hood" of thicker fur over his head and shoulders. He held his little red coat together across his chest with tiny skinny paws, and his great round eyes looked from one to the other with a plain appeal.

"Does he want something to eat?" asked Scroby, sitting up.

"Since you are so kind as to ask, Cousin," said Charles, "he is asking leave to finish my glass of claret."

"Carry on," said Scroby, addressing the monkey. "Go for it, then."

"Thank the gentleman, Ulysses," said Charles.

Ulysses stood up, took his cap off with one paw, laid the other over his heart, and bowed deeply towards Scroby. He then picked up the claret glass, still half full, and swallowed the wine slowly with every appearance of delight. When it was all gone he set down the glass carefully, sprang into Charles' arms, and clung to his coat collar.

"He is a spoilt beast," said James, not unkindly.

"I'd forgotten Wilkins," said Scroby suddenly. "I suppose he is all right?"

"When I went to fetch your brandy, Cousin," said Charles, "your excellent manservant was holding his head under a cold-water tap. I did not disturb him, no, sir. If he is too delicate-minded to see us in the act of materializing, the least I can do is to pretend not to see him at an inopportune moment."

"Poor Wilkins," said Scroby. "He'll never forgive himself—"

The door opened and Wilkins walked in. His face was shining from recent washing and his hair was sleeked down with water, but his manner was exactly as it should be. He came to the table and took up the tray.

"Should I refill the glasses, sir? I am sorry, sir, that there appear to be no decanters in this hotel for the use of guests. Is it your wish that I should obtain some when the shops reopen in the morning, sir?"

"Yes, do," said Scroby. "A little more claret, Cousin James-Cousin Charles?"

"Thank you, not at the moment," said James.

"Nor for me, thank you," said Charles.

Wilkins stood his ground like a man and looked straight at Ulysses.

"And the little creature, sir? Fruit, or nuts, or—"

"He adores bananas, Wilkins," said Charles, beaming upon him, "but I think he does not require anything at the moment."

"Very good, sir," said Wilkins. He collected the glasses and left the room.

"Excellent," said James. "I believe it to have been the great Duke of Wellington who said, 'Never apologize,' was it not?"

"Wilkins thinks so, anyway, and how right he is," said Scroby.

"Charles," said James Latimer, "if our cousin will not think us unmannerly, let us walk abroad a little. It will be pleasant to stroll again upon the boulevards as night falls and the lights come up in the streets."

"I am with you, James. Besides, we have yet to find somewhere to lodge. Yes, Cousin Richard, as you were about to ask when Ulysses interrupted you, while we are materialized we eat and drink and get sleepy and go to bed like any other men. We must find somewhere reasonably adjacent so that we may see you fairly often, if your patience will permit, Cousin."

"Oh, please—" said Scroby.

"It is one of the conditions of our state," explained James, "that we have to remain reasonably close to some blood-relation or we are liable to thin out and become semitransparent."

"Or, at least, plaguey dim round the edges," said Charles.

"One cannot walk about Paris going dim round the edges," said James reasonably. "It would not be fitting. It would distress the ladies. You would not have us go about distressing ladies, Richard, of that I am assured."

"Heaven forbid," said Scroby emphatically. "Women make me nervous enough in the ordinary way, but when they start getting distressed they terrify me."

"Curious," said James, deeply interested. "There must be some reason—"

"Oh, there is," said Scroby, "but never mind that now. Would this hotel suit you? I don't know whether they have room, but it doesn't seem over-full to me."

"We will enquire," said Charles, making for the door. "Let us go, James, and see to it, for nothing could be better. Richard, you are a good fellow, yes, sir, and I am happy to know you. Come, James."

They went out together—Ulysses seemed to have disappeared—and had no difficulty in engaging adjacent rooms on the floor above Scroby's. When that was settled they strolled out together in the evening light, looking contentedly about them. There was an inconspicuous man lounging in a doorway almost opposite to the Lune d'Italie; the cousins crossed the road and came almost face to face with him. He had a cap pulled down over his eyes and did not look up as they passed, but they both looked at him and then glanced at each other.

James wrinkled his nose as though he had seen something unpleasant and Charles said: "You are in the right, Cousin."

"But, I trust, no concern of ours."

"I am of your mind, James. But, my stars, what a specimen!"

They strolled on together.

Pépi the Crocodile and his friend Jules were sitting at a café table drinking small glasses of a colorless fluid which would have taken the skin off throats less pachydermatous than theirs, and waiting for Fingers Dupré. He was a particularly inconspicuous man, as a pickpocket needs to be, and he had gone to the Lune d'Italie to see if he could pick up any information about Richard Scroby. Jules was idly watching the passersby when Pépi, who was reading a newspaper, uttered an exclamation.

"What is it?" asked Jules.

"Toni le Chat. Those—English police have charged him with that double murder in Highgate."

"We knew they would," said Jules.

"Yes, I know, but listen. 'The accused was carried into Court as he is suffering from a broken ankle sustained at the time of his arrest.' I told you so. That Scroby, he is police. He rushed downstairs and arrested Toni."

"Here comes Fingers," said Jules.

Fingers sidled up to the table, for it was one of his peculiarities that he seldom faced squarely towards the direction in which he was going. He sat down and looked pointedly at Pépi's glass.

"Will you never buy a drink for yourself?" grumbled Pépi.

"Not on business."

Pépi sighed and gave in. When the drink had been brought he leaned across the table and said: "Well?"

"He is there," said Fingers, "the man Scroby, at the Lune d'Italie. He has a suite on the first floor and there is also the manservant. He has also two friends."

"Friends?"

Fingers nodded.

"English, also?"

"They think, one English, one American, but they speak French well. Scroby, not so well." Fingers sipped from his glass.

"As friends of Scroby's, are they of any account?" asked Jules. "Could one brush them off if they gave trouble?"

Fingers stared down at his glass. "I wouldn't."

"Wouldn't what? Try to brush them off? Why? Are they tough—do they carry arms—what's the matter?"

"Don't know," said Fingers impassively, and Jules lost patience.

"Put the wind up you, have they?" But Fingers neither moved nor answered. "Who are they, judges or some such?"

"Fingers," said Pépi after a short silence, "tell us what you know. What's the matter with those two?"

"Don't know," said Fingers again.

"Oh, scrub it," said Jules impatiently. "What's it matter? It's only to get the Englishman by himself; we don't need to mix it with those two."

Fingers nodded and agreed to go on watching the place.

"For I am afraid," said Pépi, "that Scroby may know me and I am sure that that manservant saw Jules in London. You, Fingers, are the sort of man no one notices."

"Those two," said Fingers, "they noticed me."

CHAPTER VII
He Blamed the Fish

JAMES LATIMER looked up as his cousin Charles came into the room, Charles' bedroom on the second floor of the Lune d'Italie.

"Well, Charles? Did you learn from Richard what this matter is with which we have been sent to deal?"

Charles shook his head. "He says he can think of nothing, James, and Richard is as truthful a man as ever stepped in shoe leather, I will go bail upon it. He says that he cannot charge his mind with having offended any and that, if he had, why should he be in danger? For men do not, in these days, avenge with violence an unintended slight. I asked if he were connected with any organization, such as the police, which might earn him ill will, and he says not. The only suggestion he could make is that some accident may be about to befall him from which we may save him." Charles laughed. "I would not like to avow that that suggestion was made seriously, no, sir. I think our young cousin finds the idea diverting."

James smiled indulgently. "He is an ingenuous youth and refreshingly lighthearted. It must, then, be something of which he is unaware. He seems to be comfortably well-to-do, can it be that someone hopes to inherit if he were to join us?"

"I thought of that," said Charles, lighting a cigarette, "but not of an inoffensive way of putting the question."

"Difficult," said James, "difficult. I see your point. We can, then, but wait until we are directed—"

"I think," interrupted Charles, "I am not sure, but I think that the excellent Wilkins might be able to help us. He was about the room while we were talking and it seemed to me that he caught my eye with meaning."

"We will speak with Wilkins when Richard is not there."

"He is not there at the moment, Cousin James, he has gone out to hunt snuffboxes."

"Snuffboxes? But I understood that gentlemen no longer used snuff."

"You are in the right, James, yes, sir. So much so that a snuffbox is now become a curio and collectors vie with each other to possess choice specimens. Our Richard is such a collector."

James got up. "Let us go down, Charles, and speak with Wilkins. So Richard collects snuffboxes. I remember collecting birds' eggs when I was a boy."

"And I, snakeskins. I was mighty proud of my collection."

They left the room and walked along the corridor to the stairs.

"What else does Richard do in his leisure?"

"Boxing, James, boxing. The manly art of fisticuffs. He will not speak of his prowess but admits that he enjoys it, from which I calculate that he must be a good man of his hands. No man could honestly enjoy being always knocked flat and having his claret tapped."

"I fought a practice round once with Jem the Bruiser," said James, to Charles' surprise. "Cousin, I thought one of your American tornados had overtaken me."

They knocked at Scroby's door and Wilkins opened it.

"I am so sorry, gentlemen, Mr. Scroby has gone out."

"We know it, my good man," said James. "It was you with whom we wished to have a few words."

"Very good, sir," said Wilkins, holding the door wide. The Latimers entered the sitting room and sat down while Wilkins stood before them.

"You know," began James, "that we are no longer mortal."

"Yes, indeed, sir."

"We were permitted to return because, as we were informed, your master had need of our help."

"Indeed, sir?"

"We naturally expected to find him in some difficulty or embarrassment which weighed upon him, but he seems to have no consciousness of any such thing."

"No, sir. A cheerful and carefree young gentleman, Mr. Scroby, if I may be allowed to say so."

"Wilkins," said Charles, "you were in the room during some of the time when I was trying to strike oil in this matter and I thought—maybe I mistook you—I thought you had something you could say. Yes, sir, I thought there was a gleam in your eye, if you understand me."

"Well, sir—"

"Come clean, Wilkins."

"Well, sir, it is hardly my place to comment upon the family, but there is Mr. Scroby's aunt, sir."

"Proceed, Wilkins."

"She intends to marry him, sir."

This brought James out of his chair.

"What—what—it's impossible. Ridiculous. Preposterous. You must be mistaken."

"I beg your pardon, sir, for inadvertently misleading you. Miss Scroby does not, of course, intend to marry Mr. Scroby herself. What she means to do is to unite him in the bonds of matrimony with a Miss Millicent Biggleswade, sir."

"Miss—"

"Millicent Biggleswade. The young lady is a daughter of the Rector of the village where Miss Scroby lives. It is in Surrey, sir. I understand that Miss Scroby is Miss Biggleswade's godmother, sir, and that Miss Biggleswade has been greatly under Miss Scroby's influence since her infancy. Miss Biggleswade's infancy I would be understood to mean."

"I follow your meaning, Wilkins," said Charles.

"Thank you, sir. A very forceful lady, Miss Scroby, sir. With perfect respect, a lady of strong character."

"One of those driving forces one hears about," suggested Charles.

"Precisely, sir. If I may be permitted to say it, sir, I think Miss Scroby desires the marriage because then she would retain a certain hold over Mr. Scroby both direct and, as it were, through his wife. Whereas if my master were to marry some independent young lady—"

"They would both cut loose?"

"I regard it as highly probable, sir. My young gentleman is of a most estimable character and I must say that I have never had the least trouble with him, sir, but he is not by nature of a sufficiently rocklike and stubborn character to resist such pressure as Miss Scroby brings to bear. She— she'll have him married in the end, sir, I know it, I can see it coming!"

"But if he selected a life's partner for himself as every man has a right to do," said James, "what then?"

"She would somehow contrive to blight the young romance, sir. Mr. Scroby has once or twice displayed a natural interest in quite suitable young ladies but, when confronted with her, they paled and fled, sir."

"Most unfortunate," said James.

"Yes, sir. I might perhaps add that this visit to Paris is the very first time that he has rebelled, sir. For the first time in his life, so he tells me, Miss Scroby does not know his address, or even that we are in Paris."

"Indeed. This Miss Biggleswade, Wilkins, what is she like?" asked Charles.

Wilkins raised his eyebrows and clasped his hands lightly together in front.

"Meek, sir. Amiable. A quiet young lady, sir, doesn't say much. Arranges flowers. Plays the piano a little. Takes a class in Sunday school— the infants, sir. Calls Miss Scroby 'Aunt Angela,' sir."

"Oh, hell," said Charles. "The `shape of things to come'?"

"I could not say, sir."

"I really meant," said Charles, "what is she like in appearance?"

Some sort of emotion appeared through the formal mask of the well-trained manservant but, whatever it was, Wilkins quelled it. After only the briefest pause:

"Undistinguished, sir."

"But has she no hobbies?" asked James. "For a person's chosen favorite pursuits are as indicative of character as any. What is it that she likes best of all?"

"Suet pudding, sir, preferably with treacle."

"Gentlemen, hush," said Charles. "No wonder our young cousin fled to Paris."

Wilkins moved his right hand over his left instead of having the left hand over the right.

"What actually precipitated our abrupt departure, gentlemen, was not, if I may make myself clear, Mr. Scroby's matrimonial prospects. What actually triggered off the explosion, if I may so put it, was the publicity, gentlemen. Mr. Scroby is constitutionally averse to newspaper publicity."

"What—"

"Excuse me one moment, gentlemen."

Wilkins retired to his own room and came back a few moments later with a newspaper in his hand.

"I must apologize, gentlemen, the newspaper is a little creased. I brought it over in my luggage, gentlemen."

The paper was the *Daily Megaphone* of the day when Scroby had crossed to Paris, and the Latimers bent together over the front page, reading the headlines aloud in antiphonal chant.

"Toni le Chat Captured—Clubman Fells Him with Vase—'I merely went straight to bed'— Good gracious me, Wilkins!"

"Precisely, sir."

The cousins read on. "Mr. Richard Scroby, well known to connoisseurs as a collector of snuffboxes, described to our representative how he had foiled an impudent attempt at burglary which was doubtless aimed at some of his more valuable specimens. Mr. Scroby returned to his flat after dining out and was on the point of switching on the light when he saw, silhouetted against the lights outside, the head and shoulders of a man in the act of climbing in at the window. Mr. Scroby immediately snatched up a tall and heavy Japanese vase which stood on a table nearby and struck the intruder so shrewd a blow on the head that the man lost his hold upon the windowsill and fell to the ground some twenty feet below, breaking his ankle and sustaining cuts and contusions.

" 'I was tired.'

"Mr. Scroby, having 'repelled boarders' in the best traditions of the British Navy, then lost interest in the fracas and retired to bed. He was, he said, tired and the man was gone, so why worry?

"The porter, having heard a sound outside and someone groaning, went to investigate and found the man lying helpless on the ground. He summoned the police, who came within minutes of the call and then discovered, upon investigation, that the man was a well-known cat burglar of French origin called Toni le Chat who was 'wanted' on suspicion of being concerned in the particularly brutal murder of an elderly couple at Highgate who, it is suggested, may have disturbed him in the act of rifling their safe.

"It is understood that Toni le Chat had two or more associates who are said to have assisted him in his alleged crimes. The police are now on the trail of these men and further arrests may be expected shortly.

"It is hoped that an end may now be put to a series of violent crimes which have—"

The Latimers lifted their eyes from the newspaper.

"Where were you, Wilkins, while all this was happening?"

"Unfortunately, sir, not there. Mr. Scroby had kindly given me permission to spend the night with my married sister at Dorking, sir."

"I guess, Wilkins," said Charles, "that this bunch took the trouble to worm out of someone that you were going to be away that night before they planned this affair."

"That may well be, sir. Mr. Scroby was so good as to say the same thing when I blamed myself for being absent, sir, upon that inauspicious occasion."

"Mr. Scroby seems to have managed quite well single-handed," said Charles. "Yes, sir, I opine that he dealt very capably with the emergency, how say you, Cousin?"

"Yes, indeed," said James. "There is an underlying suggestion in this account that Mr. Scroby had—er—dined rather well that night. It is nearly impertinent."

"Mr. Scroby had returned from a dinner of the Old Boys of his school, sir. He admitted not feeling very well; he blamed the fish, sir."

As the days passed, Miss Scroby, at home in England, became increasingly uneasy about nephew Richard's welfare. It will be remembered that she had left him surrounded by reporters, police, and others, in order to inspect another flat in the same block. When she had done this she returned to Scroby's flat and was disconcerted to receive no answer to her ringing. When she was tired of pressing a button and hearing only a faint buzz within, she went down to the hall and interviewed the porter, who told her that Scroby, Wilkins, and luggage for two had departed by taxi for an unknown destination.

"Did you not hear where he directed the taxi to go?"

"No, madam."

"Nor see the labels on the luggage?"

"No, madam. I am sorry—"

"It does not matter," she said, and walked away thinking that it showed the right feeling in Richard if he had fled from publicity and that no doubt he would write to her from wherever he had gone. Probably to Cornwall;

Richard always went to Cornwall.

However, the days passed without bringing even the practically statutory picture-postcard with the usual message: "Good journey, arrived safely, weather magnificent," but not, since Scroby was inherently truthful, "Wish you were with me." Miss Scroby became the prey of misgivings; she thought of Toni le Chat's criminal accomplices and shuddered; she thought of the nylon stocking embroidered with cupid's hearts and ground her teeth. Vicious men or fast women, it could be either, and he a Scroby! Something must be done and there was none but her to do it. She caught the ten-fifteen to Waterloo.

At the flats, the porter had no news of Mr. Scroby. No, madam, he had left no forwarding address for letters and in any case there had been no letters.

"No letters! But I have written to him myself."

"It 'asn't come 'ere, madam."

"Very odd. Oh, I suppose he has left a forwarding address at the post office."

"I could not say, madam."

"Where is your nearest post office?"

"Round to the right, madam, and across the main road."

"Thank you."

But the local post office, loyally abiding by its rules, refused to give any information on Scroby's whereabouts. A letter, directed to his usual address, would be forwarded and that was all.

Miss Scroby stood herself lunch in a local Lyons' and read a paper which had been discarded by a previous occupant of her place. It was, actually, a copy of the *Daily Megaphone* and she skimmed disapprovingly through it till she came to the advertisement column headed Personal. "Stolen, on the evening of May 29th, a Mink Coat, a Solitaire Diamond Ring—" "Prepare to meet thy Doom." "Is your hair thinning on top?" "Pogo, adored one, where are you?" "Discipline your Diaphragm with Diulytrium." "Percival, Perkins and Pink, confidential enquiries with the utmost tact—"

"Ha," said Miss Scroby thoughtfully.

She took a shopping list from her handbag and made a note of an address.

CHAPTER VIII
Winter Circus

THE COOKING at the Lune d'Italie was passable but not inspired; also, the small tables were too far apart, so that one tended to talk only with one's table companion. James and Charles Latimer had acquired the habit of taking at least one meal a day at the Café Grecque, where the tables are packed so closely together that it is not merely easy to fall into conversation with strangers, it is practically impossible to avoid it. The members of the International Press Agency go there, so do many French people who appreciate good cooking; so also do English and American visitors from nearby hotels.

Hawkes the journalist was an habitué when in Paris, but he had been away for some days doing articles about the annual fête days in which Brittany so rightly rejoices, and the Latimers had not met him. They strolled into the Grecque for lunch to receive the usual cheerful greeting from the waiter and sidle into chairs at a small table in the further room. The place was crowded and rang with chatter; on one side of them a French businessman was talking about paper to a Belgian friend, on the other side two young lovers leaned across their table till their faces nearly met, and murmured together.

James sat down and looked pleasedly about him.

"One would say, Charles, that all the world travels. Here we find a fair selection from the disaster at the Tower of Babel as told in Holy Writ."

Charles inclined his ear.

"Too wide a selection for me. Yes, sir, I opine that many of those present are very far from home. Would that be Swedish, at the next table but one?"

James listened for a moment.

"One of the Germanic languages," he said, "but I cannot distinguish. Back to back with you—"

The waiter came and took their order, or began to do so, for the Frenchman and the Belgian at the next table rose to go and two ladies who had just entered the café saw a vacant table and swooped upon it.

"This table will do for us very well, Virginia. Waiter, is this table engaged for anyone?"

The waiter spoke little or no English, but the gesture and the query were unmistakable. At a sign from James he abandoned the Latimers to draw out the table so that the elder woman could pass round it and sit down on the padded seat against the wall while the younger sat facing her and consequently beside Charles, who stood until the ladies were settled and then sat down to study the menu. The waiter removed the debris left by the previous clients from the ladies' table with, apparently, one sweep of the hands, spread a clean cloth, handed them both a copy of the menu, and returned to the Latimers. By the time they had ordered, the ladies were ready.

The elder called up the waiter with a lifted finger. "Do you speak English?"

The waiter raised his hands in apology. "A word, three words—I am sorry."

"Oh dear. Then he must just put up with my French. I don't think they taught me so well at school."

The girl laughed. "Go to it, Mother! I guess it isn't that we don't use the right words but we don't seem to say them right. Either that, or they don't."

"Well, it's their language," said her mother doubtfully. She then drew herself up and explained, in French which would probably have been perfectly good if it had been written down, that her digestion would not tolerate anything made with vinegar or even lemon. Nothing acid, nothing. Not even a trace, used in cooking. The waiter listened with strained attention and gathered some of it.

"No vinegar, madame," and he took the vinegar bottle out of the cruet. The lady was so pleased that she nodded vigorously, so he put it back again.

"I don't mind it on the table," she said, "it's in the food that it kills me. You tell him, Virginia."

Virginia was dark-haired, bright-eyed, extremely pretty and about nineteen. She did her best and the waiter took the vinegar bottle out again. Virginia said slowly and with great care that the bottle was quite all right in the cruet-stand, they didn't mind it standing there at all so long as it wasn't *there,* and she poked the menu with a slim pink finger.

The waiter snatched up the menu, which was, in fact, quite unspotted; rubbed it fiercely with his napkin and banded it back. Charles leaned his head in his hands and James murmured to him across the table.

"Should you not rescue your fellow countrywomen from their

predicament?"

Charles straightened his face with an effort and turned to the elderly lady with a polite bow.

"Ma'am, excuse me, if my little knowledge of French would be of service—"

"Oh, now, isn't that kind. I'm sure you must have heard what I was trying to tell this waiter; I just can't take vinegar in anything, it just kills me, and you never know what's in all these sauces, do you? So delicious, but it's absolute murder to me—"

Charles explained matters to the waiter in fluent French which the man understood perfectly although the accent was a little strange to him; a soft slow drawl with some of the syllables oddly accented and some of the words sounding old-fashioned to his ear, for Charles spoke the French of New Orleans which derives from the time when France was a kingdom with a Louis on the throne. The waiter bowed and said that he understood perfectly and doubtless the poor madame was a sufferer from the gastric ulcer, and he patted his midriff. The stomach, what it gives one to endure.

With Charles' help, an innocuous meal was ordered for the lady; her daughter was much easier to please.

"Well, now," said the lady, "if that's what you call a little knowledge of French I guess mine is just not here at all. It is so embarrassing. I mean, I'm so ashamed of myself, because back home I was reckoned to be quite good at it. I mean, I can read French so easily, it's no trouble at all, but talking it over here, well! What I want is to go back to school." Virginia laughed and her mother turned on her. "And you're no better, so we'd best go back to school together."

"Yes, Mother," said Virginia, dimpling. "What they call a finishing school, I guess?"

Her mother turned a smiling face to the Latimers, a naturally pleasant face with handsome dark eyes and gray hair perfectly dressed. "My daughter," she said. "is amused at her poor mother getting stuck like that; it's too bad, isn't it?"

James bowed. "I am assured, ma'am, that you and your charming daughter are the most delightful companions together."

"We rub along," laughed Virginia, "we rub along very well."

"As for your difficulties with the language, ma'am," said Charles, "it is only a question of practice, believe me. A week, or maybe ten days, and suddenly you will find that you both speak and understand perfectly. Like a miracle, yes, ma'am, that is how it will be."

"Well, I'm sure I hope so. Excuse me, but you are an American, are you not?"

"I am, yes, ma'am. I come from that state for which your daughter is so delightfully named."

"Well now, isn't that interesting, and so do I. We must get together about Virginia. But you," turning to James, "are English, are you not?"

"That is so, ma'am, but although we are of different nationalities and born three thousand miles apart, we are cousins."

"I see, yes, and you are traveling together, isn't that nice?"

Charles turned to the girl. "May I ask, ma'am, where in Virginia has the good fortune to be your home?"

"Oh, just a little place near Charlottesville, very quiet, very pretty, but a bit remote, you know? And you?"

"I come from Shandon, ma'am," said Charles, his face and his voice softening as they always did when he spoke of his home. "Shandon, near Richmond, a small place of no particular importance, no, ma'am, but very pleasant to remember. One main street with the cottonwood trees lining the sidewalks; a few dusty lanes leading off into the country districts around. Main Street widens, ma'am, towards the south because the Episcopal Church is in the middle of the road, an old red brick church, ma'am, with a white clapboard belfry and a clock with four faces, and the chimes play 'Bells of Shandon' at every hour." Charles' dark eyes looked away past the girl at some far-distant scene. "It is a long time since I was there, a long time." He broke off suddenly and looked straight at her. "I must apologize, ma'am, it is your lovely name which has made me forget my manners, yes, ma'am. Tell me, are you making some stay in Paris?"

"I am here to study antiques," she said, "old silver mostly. You have been in Paris some time, have you? You are staying here?"

"Not for long, ma'am, no, only a short visit."

"Then your home is in England, with your cousin, maybe?"

"No, in France. In a small village north of Rheims."

"That surely is unusual," said Virginia, "an Englishman and an American living together in a small village in northern France."

Charles' long mouth curled up irrepressibly at the corners. "We do not, in fact, live there, ma'am, not to speak precisely."

"I think you are just being mysterious," she said with a smile, and her mother intervened.

"Virginia, dear! The questions that girl asks, she should be an examiner of some kind."

"You are studying antiques," said James. "Do you attend classes—visit museums and collections of various kinds?"

"Museums," said Virginia, "and collections, as you say. I like museums, and collections, and the junk-boxes down by the Seine, and secondhand shops and scruffy curio dealers and the Flea Market on a Sunday morning—"

"And what else?" laughed Charles.

"Eating in cafés and military bands marching and *marrons glacés* and clowns in circuses and going on the Seine in a *bateau mouche* and the fountains in the Place de la Concorde and night clubs and concerts of classical music and the view from the Eiffel Tower—"

"Delightful," said James, "delightful. Tell me, Miss Virginia, is there anything which you disapprove?"

"Garlic," she said, wrinkling the nose, "and I have my doubts about French plumbing."

"They are justified," said James darkly. "I beg your pardon, ma'am, you were about to speak?"

"I was going to say that I'm not so keen on Virginia wandering around these galleries all alone, or running about Paris unescorted," said Virginia's mother.

"Oh, Mother, we've been over all that. I'm quite capable of looking after myself."

"That may be, but," to James in an undertone, "she is much too young."

"And too pretty," said James in the same tone.

"And these miles of museums, they kill me. Tell me, why do museums just have to have marble floors?"

"We have a young cousin staying at our hotel," said Charles, "who' is fanatical about museums, yes, ma'am. I opine his idea of heaven is an endless line of glass cases displaying snuffboxes, how say you, James?"

"Is he a young boy, then?"

"A young man," said Charles. "His name is Richard Scroby, warranted sound in wind and limb, quiet to ride or drive, well mannered and steady in traffic. May we present log him for your approval, ma'am, upon some convenient occasion?"

"Do," said the elder woman, "do. I'd certainly like to meet your cousin if he has all those virtues. Our name, by the way, is Townsend, and yours, I take it, is Scroby?"

"No, Latimer," said James, and introduced Charles and himself.

"We'll surely come here again," said Mrs. Townsend, "if only because here's the one waiter in all Paris who knows what I can't eat." She gathered up gloves and handbag. "You come in here often, do you? Then we'll meet again, maybe tomorrow if I'm not worn down to the knees treading marble halls. Virginia, couldn't we just go for a nice drive some place this afternoon? It's a shame to waste the sunshine. Good-bye, Mr. Latimer, good-bye, Major Latimer, and thanks so much for all your help. We'll be meeting again right soon."

"Now that," said James when the ladies had gone, "is the right sort of girl for Richard."

"Cousin, I am of your opinion, yes, sir. I remember the name of Townsend," said Charles, "a good old Virginian family."

"Excellent," said James politely, "excellent," for he always found it difficult to believe that Virginia was old enough to hold any "good old" families except, of course, his own relations who happened to have gone there. "I imagine," he went on, "that we shall find this matter of Richard Scroby's marriage to be what we are sent here to achieve. To avert a loveless match is an object well worth our attention and may prevent untold harm to future generations. We need not to be anxious," said James placidly, "we shall receive guidance when we need it."

A few evenings later, a group of five people dined early at the Café Grecque before going out together.

"We shall require two taxis," said James Latimer, "otherwise the ladies will be intolerably constricted for space."

"That's right," said Scroby, a little nervously. "Mustn't overcrowd the ladies." He edged away from the elder lady, who alarmed him. A tendency to manage things.

"We'd best walk down to the Boulevard des Capucines, then," said Virginia Townsend. "We'll never get two taxis at once in this street and they just can't wait. Besides, they're all going the wrong way."

"Traffic in one-way streets is always going the wrong way," said Charles Latimer. "Miss Virginia, ma'am, don't ask me why, but from my own observation that is so. How say you, Mrs. Townsend, ma'am?"

"Don't ask me, for I wouldn't know, the most of the time I don't know which way I want to go, and at night it's worse. Major Latimer, when the lights go on all colors, I tell you Paris just whirls around me."

"Disconcerting, ma'am," smiled Charles.

"And this Cirque d'Hiver, which I take it means the Winter Circus, why is it running in June, can you tell me that? Or do they do it on ice?"

The Latimers and their guests arrived at the Cirque d'Hiver in good order and were shown to their seats as the show began. Magnificent white horses with acrobats using their broad backs as platforms, jugglers, clowns, performing seals, a trampoline act, six trained monkeys practically airborne upon the flying trapeze—

Charles leaned forward to catch the eye of James, who raised his eyebrows and looked a little nervous; Charles smiled and Mrs. Townsend asked him if the joke was a private one.

"No, ma'am, no. It is an old story against us that where we are there is usually, sooner or later, a monkey. As here. Yes, ma'am, my cousin and I seem just naturally to attract the society of monkeys."

"Coincidence, of course, and it could so easily be something worse than a troupe of performing monkeys. There's a charming young girl back home, the daughter of a very dear friend of mine, and believe it or not, Major Latimer, wherever that poor girl goes there's someone has hiccups—the loud kind. I tell you, when we hear someone giving strangled squeaks in a bus or a concert-room or at church, we have only to look around and there's Linda. She's a real sweet girl, too. I know her mother's worried. I told her it was only coincidence and coincidences don't go on happening, but this surely is a tough one. I mean, Linda's a very attractive girl indeed, but any man'll think twice about matrimony if he's going to spend his married life making noises like a teddy bear with a squeak in it."

"Yes, ma'am, that certainly is tough," sympathized Charles. "I'd say there might be a case for a Minister of Religion doing some kind of exorcism."

But a set of performing lions came on to replace the monkeys, whose act had been carried through without any interference or mishap, and James breathed a sigh of relief.

The monkey act left the ring in good order, six of them filing out with their trainer walking beside them. No one noticed a seventh little monkey skipping away in the shadows; Ulysses, strengthened and invigorated by the presence of his kind, able and willing to go about and enjoy himself.

He began by going up to the staff bar, which was occupied by the bartender, the seal trainer, and a couple of jugglers all engaged in discussing a new turn which one of them had seen somewhere. This man put down a half-empty glass of red wine to demonstrate what he had seen; he was in the middle of the act when he was interrupted by an exclamation from the bartender.

"Don't interrupt," said the juggler irritably, "you put me off.

"But, look," said the bartender, pointing.

Ulysses was sitting on the bar with the juggler's wineglass held carefully in both hands and the last of the wine was just disappearing down his throat. The juggler aimed a slap at him, but Ulysses dropped the glass on the bar and leapt away out of sight.

"That's one of Ricardo's animals got loose," said the other juggler mournfully. "There'll be trouble over this."

"But Ricardo's monkeys aren't dressed," said the seal trainer. "Only just their own fur."

"That one," said the bartender, "had a jacket and a cap."

"Another shot, please," said the juggler who had been robbed. "And in a clean glass; you can wash that one."

"I've never seen Ricardo's monkeys," said the other juggler. "I don't demean myself looking at animal acts. No skill. No athleticism. No natural gifts at all."

"Thirty francs, please," said the bartender.

"Ricardo will pay," said the juggler.

"That wasn't Ricardo's monkey—"

"Must have been. Only monkeys here."

"Ricardo's monkeys aren't dressed—"

"That one was—"

CHAPTER IX
I Smell Danger

ULYSSES, warm, vigorous, and glowing, capered away to find some further amusement. He glanced at the ring through the animal entrance, but there were only dogs there and Ulysses did not care for dogs. He found a room of which the door was ajar and peered carefully round the corner; the room seemed to be empty, but there were sounds of movement from a square box on the floor. The box had a barred front; Ulysses crept round and peered in. Inside the box was the biggest barnyard rooster he had ever seen in his life and in magnificent condition. The bird was, of course, one of the acts; he answered any question involving the use of numbers by dabbing with his beak at a series of cards, numbered 0 to 9, laid out in a semicircle round him. He was short-tempered, haughty, and very proud of himself.

Ulysses said "Eek!" The cock—a Buff Orpington—looked at him first with one eye and then the other and made a rude noise in his throat, so the monkey walked round the box and examined it. There was a door at the back, closed with a hasp and staple to take a padlock, though at that moment the padlock was not there. Ulysses, after a few false starts, pulled the hasp clear of the staple and opened the door. The rooster looked round but did not come out; Ulysses, who, like all monkeys, had no patience, seized a double handful of feathers and tugged.

The rooster uttered a screech of rage, flew at the monkey, and pecked him enough to hurt; Ulysses was not used to violence and lost his temper. He slapped the bird across the face, chattering with fury, grabbed it by the tail, and pulled. The rooster immediately panicked and rushed, shrieking, out of the room, upsetting a bottle of beer and scattering straw and paper in his flight. Towing Ulysses behind him, he made straight for the ring and burst into general view at the moment when the performing dogs had arranged themselves in the balanced pyramid which was the end of their act.

The Buff Orpington screeched and ran, flapping; dust flew; the audience stood up the better to see what was coming, and Ulysses hung on like grim death, scattering tail feathers which, one by one, gave way under the strain. Round the ring they went until they passed under the noses of the pyramid of dogs who looked round sharply, lost their balance, broke formation, reverted to nature, and set off in happy pursuit. The small dogs yapped, the terriers barked madly, and the two large dogs, who had formed the base of the pyramid, bellowed after. They circled the ring twice to the enthusiastic cheers of the spectators, then the rooster jumped the fence and went off up one of the alleyways running up between the seats like the widely spaced spokes of a wheel, and the pack in full cry followed behind.

They went round the gangway at the top, down the next gangway, over the fence at the bottom, and back into the ring. By this time the arena staff were all there and they formed up and shepherded the hunt into the Performers' Exit, where they disappeared from view, but the audience cheered, stamped, and shouted "Encore" for several minutes until the stately elephants marched on to restore the dignity which had been so regrettably lost.

The owner of the rooster, which was still hysterical and largely tailless, met the owner of the dogs, which had been caught and returned to their kennels.

"Here, you," said the dog trainer furiously, "what the hell d'you mean letting your bird out, messing up my act?"

"I didn't," howled the fowl owner, "I never let him out. My Pythagoras, he is ruined, he has no tail, my act is ruined, I am ruined, all is lost. How can I show a cock with no tail? The company will laugh the place down every time he turns round— Whose monkey was that?"

"Ricardo's, of course. My dogs—"

"Ricardo, of course! My cock—"

"Come," said the dog trainer grimly. "We will go and pay a little visit to Monsieur Ricardo."

When they reached Ricardo's room he was there, a tall thin melancholy man with a long thin black mustache. He was standing in front of the cage where his monkeys were kept, and he was counting them.

"Three and two are five, and one in the corner, six. Three, and those three, six. I only have six and there they are."

The two men burst into the room.

"You, Ricardo," said the cock owner, "you let your monkeys loose to spoil other men's acts, do you? I tell you what I will do, I will beat you till you scream and then I will tear your mustache out and throw it to your monkeys! I mock myself of your mustache!" He hopped up and down, very much after the same manner as his rooster, and made ineffectual dabs at Ricardo's face, for the cock owner was a very small man and Ricardo's mustache was almost out of reach.

"Ricardo," yelled the dog trainer, "you send your monkey to ruin my show, do you? You wait till the final pose and then you make my beautiful dogs all to fall down, eh? I make you to fall down, I pull your nose, I—"

Ricardo pushed the cock owner into the arms of the dog trainer and called Heaven to witness that he was innocent. "The bartender speak to me about a monkey who steals wine, it has a jacket on. Have mine jackets on? Look—"

"You dress him, you undress him—"

"No one has monkeys but you—"

"You lie!"

"You—!"

"I pull your nose," howled the dog trainer, and did so. Ricardo lost his temper and slapped him; the cock owner kicked Ricardo on the ankle, which gave way; Ricardo tried to save himself by clutching at the dog trainer's luxuriant forelock; both of them fell over the cock owner and all three rolled on the floor together, kicking and biting and yelling with fury, while the monkeys in the cage clung together and gibbered with fright.

There were in the ring at that time a troupe of five girl trapeze artists dressed—if that is the word—in glittering breastplates and brief pink satin shorts to the back of which, just above the hips, had been added a row of pink feathers which drooped gracefully when the girls were still and waved wildly when they were not. The girls were revolving rapidly on the various stages of the trapeze, and all eyes were upon them when one of them uttered a squeal and appeared to be repelling some attack from the rear.

Two pink feathers floated down and a sailor on leave from the French cruiser *Georges Legues* commented upon them. The girl kicked out and a small brown monkey, which had joined the troupe without invitation, tore off several more feathers and threw them away. He then advanced upon another member of the troupe.

"My goodness gracious," said Mrs. Townsend, "will you look at that? It's a monkey. Virginia, it's a monkey. It must have got away from its keeper someway. Mr. Scroby, it's a monkey up there." She seized him by the arm and shook it.

Scroby, who thought he recognized the monkey in question, was speechless; not so Virginia. She grasped Scroby by the other arm, not as urging him to action but merely as holding him down while she leaned across him.

"Mother, those girls are going to fall. Mother, there's no net. Mother, I'm going to scream. Mother—"

But the girl so unceremoniously despoiled turned upon the trapeze wire and aimed so shrewd a slap at Ulysses that he vanished immediately and was no more seen. The act finished, the clowns came on in their place, and Virginia Townsend forgot her anxieties in laughter.

A day or two later Charles and James Latimer, choosing a time when they knew Scroby to be out, took counsel of Wilkins.

"We come to you for counsel," said James. "You have known Mr. Scroby for some years as against our few days' acquaintance." He sat down upon the sofa in Scroby's sitting room and carefully cut the end off a cigar while Wilkins awaited the exact moment with a box of matches.

"Something to do with Mr. Scroby, sir? Excuse me, a light for your cigar."

"Thank you—thank you. Yes. Wilkins, you have seen Miss Virginia Townsend."

"Yes, indeed, sir."

"A very charming young lady," continued James.

"Certainly, sir."

"Young, pretty, merry and with pleasing manners," said Charles.

"All that, sir."

"In short, a pippin."

"The golden apple, sir, of what I believe are called the Hesperides, if

I may be permitted to use a poetic term."

"I congratulate you upon your choice of the expression, Wilkins."

"Thank you, sir."

"In that case," pursued Charles, "and since we are all agreed, why the heck doesn't your master agree with us? Where Miss Townsend is concerned he is almost indifferent."

"I could not say, sir. Unless his previous experience with Miss Scroby's determined advocacy of Miss Biggleswade has, as it were, rubbed a callus over the tender passion in his case, if I make myself clear, sir."

"Admirably clear," said Charles. "There is not, then, so far as you know, any unhappy passage in his recent past of which Miss Townsend might inadvertently remind him? No dark-haired schemer from whom he recoiled? No lovely American who may perhaps have snubbed him? No unfortunate association with long eyelashes or a short upper lip?"

Wilkins thought for a moment and then shook his head.

"No, sir."

"Miss Townsend," said James, "cannot in any way, however recondite, remind him of Miss Biggleswade?"

"Subject," said Wilkins warmly, "to the coincidence of both the young ladies being members of the feminine sex of *homo sapiens,* there is no resemblance at all."

"Gentlemen, hush!" said Charles. "Wilkins, speaking quite personally from your own point of view, how would you regard the prospect of Mr. Scroby's marriage?"

"That would depend entirely upon Mr. Scroby's choice of a lady, sir. If—" Wilkins hesitated.

"Go on, my good man," said James kindly.

"I was about to say, sir, that if Miss Biggleswade became Mr. Scroby's bride, my days with the family would be short indeed. Miss Scroby, sir, does not like me."

"But suppose Miss Townsend—"

"In that case, sir, a welcome as warm as is consistent with my place, sir, would confidently be forthcoming."

"Even if they wanted to go and live in America?"

"America is a great and interesting country," said Wilkins with an apologetic glance at Charles, "but I understand that there is there a marked shortage of well-trained menservants. I gather, sir, that I should find myself something of what is called a *rara avis*, sir. Almost a social asset, if I may be allowed to say so."

"Certainly. You wouldn't mind that?"

"On the contrary, sir."

"That being so," said James, "have you any suggestion to make as to how this end may be achieved and Mr. Scroby's indifference overcome?"

Wilkins smiled faintly.

"Propinquity, sir, propinquity. I understand that it seldom fails."

"In a little more detail, Wilkins—"

"Throw them together, sir. Repeatedly."

"Ah," said Charles. "Yes. Yes, indeed. I remember, when I was young, this throwing together. Most efficacious. Pleasant, too."

"Yes, sir. Er—alone together, of course. I would say, unescorted, sir."

"Naturally, Wilkins. It will not be easy, her mama is a careful guardian."

"Ingenuity, sir, will overcome all obstacles."

"I hope so," said James, putting out the stub of his cigar and rising to his feet. "Thank you for your counsel, Wilkins."

"Not at all, sir."

The Latimers went down to the bar for an *apéritif* before lunch.

"Tell me," said Charles, "if you can remember, Cousin, which evening Mrs. Townsend is engaged to spend with her ex-school friend who is passing through Paris?"

"Tonight," said James. "I think, tonight."

"I was wondering whether Miss Virginia is equally as enthusiastic as her mother upon spending the evening with an elderly lady, however charming."

"I should doubt it," said James seriously. "The awkward gap of one generation only is commonly a bar to any real community of interest, since any reminiscences the elder may have to offer have, as a rule, already been supplied by the parents. Grandparents, on the other hand, practically rank as historical personages and partake of the nature of antiquarian research."

"You always put things so well, James. I was wondering whether Miss Virginia would smile upon a suggestion that she should spend the evening with us. Some entertainment of some kind. We should, of course, include Richard in the party and I opine that we need not overpower them with our continual presence."

"So long as we are the hosts—"

"And remain hove to somewhere in the offing," said Charles.

Virginia Townsend, approached by telephone, said that it was a real lovely idea and she would adore to come, and Mother would be just delighted to have her out of the way for the evening. Scroby suggested a show near the Etoile where there was Spanish singing and dancing in quiet and seemly surroundings, to which one could take a nice girl without fear of any awkward contretemps.

"Did you hear that?" said James, aside, to Charles. "He called her 'a nice girl.' "

"Encouraging," murmured Charles. "Yes, sir. Reassuring."

Just before nine the two Latimers and Scroby came out of the Lune d'Italie and told the taxi driver to drive first to the Hôtel Scribe to pick up a lady and thereafter drive them all to a café—address given—near the Etoile. They then entered the taxi and drove away, and an inconspicuous dark figure, which had been hanging about the hotel entrance, hurried away to the nearest telephone.

The cabaret was amusing without being suggestive; the singers could sing and the dancers could certainly dance; there was a conjuror who did unbelievable things. Richard Scroby and Virginia Townsend were evenly matched in their command of the French language and they helped each other with many mistakes and much laughter. Charles and James Latimer drew their chairs a little back to talk quietly together and watch the blond head and the dark one drawing closer as the time went on.

"It is working, Cousin," murmured Charles, "it is working. The ice is now melted, how say you, James?"

James nodded. "I think we have misunderstood the problem," he said. "I believe it to be the elder ladies of whom our young cousin is terrified. The authoritative, the managing ones, not the young and light of heart."

"You are in the right, James, and I am strongly of your opinion. How say you, shall we make some excuse and leave Scroby to take her home?"

At that moment a man slipped between the tables until he reached them, leaned over them and said: "Excuse me, please. The Messieurs Latimer?"

"What is it?"

"One asks for you on the telephone, messieurs, from your hotel, the Lune d'Italie. It is said the message is urgent."

"We come," said James, and Charles bent forward to speak to Scroby.

"Someone wants us on the telephone, it seems it is urgent. If we have to go somewhere, you will take Miss Virginia home?"

"Of course, of course," said Scroby, "but can't I do anything—"

"No, no. We can manage very well indeed. But do not wait about for us."

"All right—"

"Come, Charles," said James, and they went out quickly in order not to interrupt the act.

"Follow me, messieurs, please," said the man, and led the way down a flight of stone stairs.

"The French," said James with distaste, "do keep their telephones in the oddest places."

"I know," laughed Charles, "I have noticed that before." At the bottom of the stairs there was a chilly stone-floored passage with tiled walls, naked electric lights, three or four doors ajar, and a sound of water running. The guide said: "This way, messieurs," and hurried on. Charles touched James' arm and they hung back momentarily.

"I smell danger," said Charles in a low tone.

"And I," answered James. "This man means mischief, but he cannot harm us."

"Let him try," said Charles, and laughed aloud; the man looked back in surprise and opened a heavy door at the far end.

"In here, messieurs, the telephone is along there."

The Latimers walked obligingly through the doorway and looked about them, and immediately the heavy door closed and there were sounds of locks and bolts in operation.

Charles laughed again. "The poor man and how deluded he is!"

"It would serve him right," said James severely, "if we removed ourselves from here at once and faced him again at the head of the stairs. Shall we do so, Charles?"

"Let us consider first, Cousin, with your good leave. There is danger here and that man was evil, but I cannot think the danger is for us. I think the attack is aimed at Scroby."

"And he has the girl with him!"

"No matter," said Charles. "He will have us with him also, though no one will know it, and I believe that we can deal with the matter. Well, shall we go?"

The door did not open and the locks did not even rattle, but the next moment the place was empty.

CHAPTER X
Nightmare in Paris

SCROBY was enjoying his evening. As Wilkins had said, he had occasionally thrown an interested eye over personable young women only to have the budding interest blighted by his aunt's unremitting care. But this time Miss Scroby was far away, he did not even think about her, and this girl was not only uncommonly pretty but great fun as well. A jolly evening.

Presumably the telephone call was genuine since a man had certainly delivered some message to the Latimers, but Scroby was reasonably sure that, whatever the news might be, the tactful Latimers did not mean to return. Good sports, both of them. Excellent fellows. Now he and Virginia would drive back to her hotel, alone together for the first time.

When the cabaret came to an end, they did not hurry. There was a little wine still in their glasses and there was plenty to talk about. Eventually Virginia looked at the clock and then at Scroby.

"Must we go?" he said.

"I think we should go soon. I know Mother won't go to sleep till she knows I'm in."

"Oh, dear, what a pity. Is she—is she what you'd call a worrier?"

"Not really, but she says women ought to have someone worrying about them. She says she's only going on worrying about me till I get married—if I do—and then she can dust me off and let my husband do the worrying. My father fusses around my mother to beat the band, they're rather sweet."

"Are you, then, thinking of getting married? I mean—er—soon? To anybody particular?"

"Do you mean am I engaged? Now, Richard, didn't I tell you I was studying only antiques at the moment?"

They went out of the place together and Scroby looked about for a taxi. A car pulled along the pavement from where it had been standing and came to a stop in front of them.

"Taxi, monsieur?"

Scroby looked at the car. It had no taximeter, which meant that it was what is called a "private taxi" and that he would probably be charged at least three times what the ride was worth, but Scroby was in no mood to dicker about the price. He had a mind above mere francs that evening. He opened the door and Virginia got in.

"Hôtel Scribe, first, for this lady," he said in his careful French. "Afterwards, to the Hôtel Lune d'Italie for me. Understood? And—er—drive with care."

"As conveying the best eggs, monsieur," said the driver with a grin. Scroby got in and sat down beside Virginia and the car moved off.

He found, to his mild surprise, that the girl was not in the far corner away from him; on the contrary, she was squarely in the middle of the back seat and rather on the edge of it, sitting very upright. He thought for a passing moment of faintly shocked surprise that she was sitting there to be near him, but her manner undeceived him. Miss Townsend was thinking about something else.

"What is it?" he asked. "Not comfortable?"

She glanced away from him. "Oh, I guess it's all right. Just my fancy." She smiled at him. "I'm just being silly. Wasn't it a lovely evening? I did enjoy it."

"There's something wrong, what is it?"

"I don't know, and that's honest. I just feel there's something a little eerie about this cab."

"Eerie? Well, that's easy. I'll stop him and we'll get out and take another one instead." Scroby sat up to speak to the driver, but Virginia stopped him.

"No, no, don't do that. I'm not going to let myself be silly. This is a very nice car and the driver is so careful. Not like most of them, dashing about at fifty miles an hour, missing things by inches and scaring me stiff."

"Yes, but what was it? Tell me."

"Well, it was just when I got in, I went to sit in that other corner and suddenly I felt I couldn't. So I am sitting in the middle, it's all right here."

Scroby leaned past her to look into the other corner, but there was nothing there. Their shoulders touched and quite suddenly he felt surprisingly strong and protective. It dawned upon him for the first time that he had been protected by other people all his life and that he was sick to death of it. Protecting someone else was a very different sensation. Pleasant, remarkably pleasant.

By the time they reached the Scribe they were hand in hand with no very clear idea how it had happened. The car stopped, the driver leapt out to open the door, and Richard handed Virginia out of the car.

"Wait for me," he said to the driver. "*Attendez. Ne partez pas.*"

"*Bien sûr, monsieur,*" said the driver, and looked after the two young people with an indulgent smile. He was quite willing to wait; he would cheerfully have waited half the night to get Scroby alone, for the driver was Jules and he had already waited nearly a fortnight for this happy moment.

Scroby came back ten minutes later with his head in the clouds and entered the cab with the welcoming driver holding the door for him. Scroby felt vaguely impelled to sit, like Virginia, in the middle of the seat, though he was not conscious of any particular reason for so doing. Virginia—

But it is only a few minutes' drive from the Hôtel Scribe to the Hôtel de la Lune d'Italie and it soon occurred to Scroby that they were taking a long time. He sat up and looked about him, only to realize that he had no idea where they were except that they definitely were not in the Rue Caumartin. Nothing like it. He opened his mouth to protest, but a quiet voice in his ear forestalled him.

Jules drove on and now he also had an uneasy feeling which he could not define. There was something in the seat behind him which he did not like. Once before he had felt like that about a passenger sitting behind him, but there had been nothing mysterious about his unease on that occasion, for his passenger had been holding a gun at the back of Jules' neck and had been threatening to pull the trigger if the driver did not do exactly as he was told. But, exactly. On this occasion there was nothing like that to be expected. He still believed Scroby to be some sort of a London policeman, but the English police do not normally carry firearms and certainly not when taking a pretty girl out for the evening in Paris. No, this was something different. More uncanny.

But he did expect Scroby to make a fuss when he noticed that he was being driven the wrong way, and Jules was ready with a story. What? The Lune d'Italie in the Rue Caumartin? Oh, pardon, monsieur! A thousand pardons. Jules had misunderstood Monsieur, who after all had not mentioned the name of the street, had he? Jules had thought that Monsieur referred to the Hôtel du Roi d'Italie which, as doubtless Monsieur knew, was just off the Quai d'Orsay. At once, monsieur, certainly, to return at once. Then the car would swing round a few corners to baffle the Englishman and proceed to its original destination. Simple.

But Scroby did not tap him on the shoulder and protest, though indeed Jules could hear him talking in the quiet tones which taxi passengers normally use when talking to each other, but this passenger was alone. He was, then, talking to himself, or rehearsing pretty speeches for the girl when next they met. Jules inclined his ear and realized that what he heard was a conversation between two people. No, not two people. Three. The voices were perfectly distinct from each other; Scroby's light and clipped in the modern manner, another much deeper and more dignified, and the third slow but, as it were, laughing, with a drawl in it. American, possibly.

The hair at the back of Jules' neck prickled. How could there be three people in the car when there had been only one to start with? They could not have entered the car later, since he had not stopped; besides, he would have heard and seen them.

They came to a well-lighted intersection where the rays of a lamp shone straight into the back of the car. Jules sat up and moved sideways so that his driving-mirror should show him the back seat and its occupants.

There was only one. There was only the man Scroby sitting in the middle with an empty space upon either hand. He must be a ventriloquist, and a good one; he should be on the halls. The other two voices spoke and Scroby turned his head from one side to the other; he was smiling slightly but his mouth was firmly closed, and at that moment the drawling voice broke into a laugh while still Scroby's lips had not moved.

Jules broke into perspiration and his hands slipped on the wheel. He lifted his foot on the accelerator; he would pull in to the pavement, stop the car, and run for it. But whatever it was in the back of the car might run after him.

He put his foot down and drove on. It was not far now and Fingers was waiting for him in the shadow of that archway; when the car drew up he would come out and be there to help him. He longed passionately for the wholesome—comparatively wholesome—presence of the silent saturnine Fingers with a length of lead pipe in his sleeve. Not far, now.

When the quiet voice spoke in Scroby's ear he started violently with surprise although he recognized it at once.

"Pray, Cousin Richard, do not be anxious. This man means mischief, no doubt about it, but Charles and I are here."

"Cousin James—"

Charles' lazy laugh, and then—

"Why, yes, Richard, both of us. When that man led us downstairs to speak on the telephone and locked us in a storeroom instead, we opined at once that his intentions were not of the best. Yes, sir, his act seemed to us to be deeply suspect."

"Locked you in a— How did you get out?"

"We just came out. Yes, sir. We are not readily to be confined, believe you me."

"Yes—no, I suppose not—"

"We owe you an apology, Richard, pray forgive us," said James Latimer. "Only the most pressing necessity could have forced us to eavesdrop upon your tête-à-tête with Miss Virginia, but—"

Scroby blushed hotly and said that it didn't matter at all, there was nothing that—er—that could—er—could not—

"Of course not, my dear boy. It is not your behavior which is subject to censure, it is ours. Our excuse is that not only did we believe you to be in some sort of danger, but your charming young friend also. Happily, our worst fears were not realized."

"But where are we going," said Scroby, "and why? Who is this driver?"

"You do not know him, Richard?" asked Charles.

"Never saw him before, so far as I know. Looks a bit of a thug, doesn't he?"

"You are not wise to your hotel having been watched for some time by a slinking rat of a fellow who skulks in doorways?"

"Heavens, no."

"Who slides after you when you go out and does his best to hear the directions you give to taxi drivers?"

"He was outside the Cirque d'Hiver, Richard," said James, "when we came out the other night with the ladies. But, if you remember, we all traveled together in the one vehicle to return home so that, if he had any evil designs upon you, they were thwarted."

"But why, why? What have I done?"

"We were warned that you were in some danger," began James, but Charles broke in.

"The excellent Wilkins let out a story which your modesty concealed. Did you not hurl forth from a window of your apartment a man who turned out to be a dangerous criminal?"

"Yes, but—"

"A Frenchman?"

"I believe so, but—"

"With two or three associates who were not caught? They, I believe, were French too. My stars, Richard, if you go about throwing criminals out of windows you can hardly complain if they bear you a grudge, no, sir."

Scroby looked from one to the other, or rather at the corners from which the voices came.

"We are by no means assured," said James, "that these men here, in

Paris, are the same gang, but if we can identify them tonight we shall be able to penetrate into their counsels, forestall their plans, and perhaps bring them down. Our suggestion appears to you feasible, Richard, does it not?"

"He is slowing down," said Charles hastily, "and there is another man lurking in that archway. Richard, into battle!"

The car slowed down and even as it drew to a stop at the curb Scroby leapt out to meet Fingers, who ran out from the dark archway. Fingers' arm went up and back, for he was armed with a short length of lead pipe, but it is a mistake to throw up even one arm when one is facing a boxer. Scroby uppercut him with all the strength at his command; Fingers rose to more than his full height and went over backwards, hitting his head against the side of the archway before falling in a heap within its shadow. He did not move at all.

Scroby turned quickly back to the car because there was still, of course, the driver to deal with and he looked to be a much tougher opponent than the other. The driver, however, seemed to be fully occupied in trying to get out of the car and not succeeding; he kicked violently and pawed the air, but his head and shoulders remained pressed against the back of the seat and his face was a mask of rage and terror.

"Can I help?" said Scroby politely.

"No, Richard, I think not. Charles and I are, I believe, fully capable of dealing with this scoundrel. You have disposed of yours?"

"Oh yes, it was easy. I only hope," said Scroby, glancing a little anxiously over his shoulder, "that I haven't broken his neck. He stuck his chin out and I couldn't resist it."

"The silly fellow," said James calmly. "Oh no, he is not dead, you need not be anxious upon that score. We should be immediately aware if he were, you know. Rest assured that he will but have a stiff neck tomorrow."

"Then—" began Scroby.

"You will do best to make your way home as fast as may be, Richard," said Charles Latimer. "I take it this neighborhood is not salubrious, no, sir, and these gentry may have more friends at call. Will you go quickly to the end of this street? There is a main road there where you may be among people and secure a taxi—"

"I'll take one with a meter this time," said Scroby, and set off, walking fast. He had a feeling that his continued presence was hindering the Latimers in their intentions, whatever they were, towards the driver, and Scroby had the greatest confidence in the Latimers.

He reached the end of the street where it entered upon a busy main road; even at this late hour there were many people about and the traffic was still considerable. Scroby paused at the corner to get his bearings; as he stood there a car came out from behind him and slowed for the turn. A pedestrian, crossing the mouth of the turning in front of the car, looked at it, stared, and then sprang for the pavement with a yelp of terror. The car drove out and away and the pedestrian, piously crossing himself, dived into an adjacent café and leaned heavily upon the bar. Scroby smiled to himself and walked briskly away.

Jules was completely terrified for almost the first time in his life, for he was much more accustomed to terrifying other people. He was not in the least imaginative, and Fingers' occasional excursions into the super-natural merely made him laugh rudely. Jules' present troubles were, there-fore, all the more shocking; these things could not be, but they were.

He received a violent push which sent him sliding away from behind the steering wheel and across the front seat, but there was no one there who could have pushed him. He struck out at his unseen assailant and merely chipped his knuckles upon the side of the door. When he tried to cling to the steering wheel his hands were wrenched off it; when he tried to kick, someone hacked him on the ankle. He made a great effort to scramble out by the other door, but powerful hands closed round his throat and half choked him. He was so terrified that he turned faint and his eyes closed; when he opened them again he found that he was being driven at a pace which, it seemed to him, would have been excessive for a fire engine. Lights flashed in his eyes and sometimes whirled about him, people seemed to be shouting, and every now and again there came the shrill sound of a traffic cop's whistle. There would be a frightful crash in a minute and he would be in the middle of it; he turned to protest to the driver—

But there was no driver. There was no one at the wheel of the car, which was then circumnavigating the Place de la Concorde. There were the famous fountains flashing in the light of the street lamps, dozens of lamps—hundreds of them—all revolving round him and throwing out sparks.

Since it is human nature to find a plausible explanation for the inex-plicable, Jules decided that he was in the grip of a nightmare. Must be.

"I understand now," he said. "I am in bed and asleep and this is all a dream." He closed his eyes firmly and hid his face in the corner of the seat.

But the next moment there was a squeal of brakes close behind him and he heard quite distinctly a raucous voice making a series of comments which were rude by any standards and not in the least dreamlike. Jules sat up as the car wriggled through gaps in the traffic on the Rue de Rivoli and shot up a street towards a crossroads ahead. There was a splintering crash as the car swopped mudguards with a van which had slowed suddenly, then the car swerved to the left, ran into some immovable object, and stopped dead. It had collided with one of those little concrete pedestals upon which Paris humanely stations its point-duty police. The idea is that a car can break its teeth on the pedestal and give the officer time to leap for his life.

Jules took in the scene with one horrified stare and then sprang out of the car and ran—and ran—and ran—

James and Charles Latimer materialized comfortably in a dark corner and strolled together along the Boulevard des Capucines towards the Rue Caumartin.

"I enjoyed that, Cousin," said Charles. "Yes, sir, I recall that I always wanted to drive through Paris and tonight I have attained my desire. Delightful."

"I am glad that you are so happy," said James. "I myself found the drive exhilarating, though I believe our passenger was not so pleased. We will go back to the hotel and await Richard; he will hardly have attained so swift a passage. We have done well tonight, Charles; we know these men now and can attend to them effectively."

"Very true," said Charles, "very true. A thoroughly successful evening. Our young cousin can use his hands, can he not? Yes, sir, I should not care to be at the receiving end of that straight right of his."

"I anticipate with particular pleasure," said James indulgently, "hearing him explain away a set of damaged knuckles to the charming Miss Virginia in the morning."

CHAPTER XI
All Work and No Pay

PÉPI, called The Crocodile on account of his wide and ready smile, had refused flatly to take any part in the abduction of Scroby.

"It is murder," he said. "Anyone who commits murder is a fool. Always, for as long as you live, murder trails after you like a bloodhound; it may never catch up with you, but any day, any moment, it may. There is an English saying, 'Murder will out,' and it is true. You do not know English, but I do. Besides," he added simply, "it is a mortal sin."

Jules jeered aloud and Fingers assumed an attitude of prayer with his eyes closed and his long hands flat together and pointing upwards before his face like a saint in a niche.

"Here endeth the first lesson," said Jules, "from the holy crocodile. You are a coward, Pépi, that is all. You crawling funk, you rat. Go back to washing dishes and scraping plates and don't get caught with your fingers in the till next time."

Pépi colored with anger. "I was framed, I tell you. I never touched the money."

"That's what all jailbirds say," said Jules. "Please, mister, it wasn't me."

For Pépi had been in the hotel business and was doing well when it was discovered that quite substantial sums of money had been missing over a period which coincided with his employment, and he went to prison, earnestly protesting his complete innocence.

The meeting broke up in disorder and Pépi left them to pursue his own calling, which was to part people from their money as pleasantly as possible. He was emphatically not a fighting man; he earned his living as a confidence trickster and his neat and harmless appearance, his good behavior, and his friendly manners were his principal assets. Not for him the unkempt hair, the unwashed hands, and the sidelong glances of the spiv; still less, of course, the battered knuckles, the shapeless nose, and the cauliflower ears of the man of violence. He quite honestly abhorred violence; it was Toni le Chat, now languishing in an English jail, who had drawn him into association with Fingers Dupré and the lumpish Jules. Now that Toni had gone it looked as though the gang were breaking up. In a way Pépi regretted this; he did not like either Jules or Fingers personally and he loathed their tendency to explode into violence, but they did provide backing of a sort; without them he would lave to stand alone, and standing alone was not in Pépi's character. He needed a stiffening of some kind, and Toni le Chat had supplied it. It was a pity about Toni le Chat.

It will be remembered that Miss Scroby, anxious and without news, had come across an advertisement of a Private Enquiry Agency, Messrs. Percival, Perkins and Pink. She made a note of the address and went straight there.

Mr. Perkins was a well-nourished little man with gray hair, gold-rimmed spectacles, and a sympathetic manner. Miss Scroby, elderly, autocratic in manner, obviously a gentlewoman and equally obviously a spinster, was a little different from the ordinary run of his clients. He looked at the good brown calf shoes, the country tweeds, the comfortable gloves, and the hat of no ascertainable date, and wondered. He settled her in a chair with some ceremony.

"Now, madam?"

"I want you to trace where my nephew has gone."

He took down all the particulars which she gave him and looked them over.

"He has been gone ten days—only ten days? Is there any reason why you should be anxious about him?"

Miss Scroby told him about Toni le Chat and his criminal associates whom, of course, the police had not caught. Perkins, who had read the case in the paper, thought that Scroby seemed perfectly capable of looking after himself but nodded and made a note. Blushing slightly, she told him about the nylon stocking on the sitting-room carpet and Perkins raised one eyebrow.

"I only want to know where he is and that he is safe and well. Here is a photograph of him."

Mr. Perkins' own opinion was that if a man of twenty-three, with plenty of money and a manservant, had never cut loose before it was high time he did. However, private detective agencies do not make a living by telling clients not to be silly. He assured her that he would put his best man on to it at once, and bowed her out.

"Probably gone to Paris," he said, instructing one of his men; "they generally do when they want to dodge their female relatives. I think it's all perfectly innocent; he probably traveled under his own passport. I don't know whether the manservant is with him or merely having his annual holiday. Try the tourist agencies first."

No difficulty or delay was encountered. Mr. Richard Scroby and his manservant had gone to Paris by air on the afternoon of the day he had left his flat. He had not booked a hotel through the travel agency.

Mr. Perkins reported this to Miss Scroby. Had Mr. Scroby friends in Paris with whom he would be likely to stay, or did Miss Scroby wish further enquiries to be made?

She did, yes. She was not aware that Mr. Scroby knew anyone living in Paris. Where was he?

Mr. Perkins' man sat down at the telephone and put calls through to a list of the Paris hotels at which a wealthy young man, complete with manservant, would be likely to stay.

The seventh hotel on the list was the Lune d'Italie in the Rue Caumartin.

When Miss Scroby was told this news she was very appreciative of Percival, Perkins and Pink's capabilities and said so, but when she sat down to think it over she was not much happier. Why should Richard have gone to Paris so suddenly and in secret when he had never been there before?

There was that nylon stocking, for a start. Plenty of perfectly respectable Englishwomen wear nylon stockings; Miss Scroby had a few pairs herself. But not, definitely not, with hearts embroidered on them, each heart transfixed with an arrow from, no doubt, Cupid's bow.

There was something painfully French about that nylon stocking.

Toni le Chat was French; that was a known fact. He had been at Scroby's flat on the same evening as the stocking, so to put it, and Richard had thrown him out of the window. Toni le Chat was a burglar and a murderer, but presumably burglars have private lives with girls in them. Richard said that he had ejected Toni le Chat because he was after the snuffboxes, but suppose Toni le Chat's visit was not professional but private. Concerned not with snuffboxes but with a girl who wore hearts on her stockings. A vulgar brawl over a French miss.

Miss Scroby's mouth tightened and her foot tapped the carpet. There were also Toni le Chat's three accomplices who had evaded the English police and probably gone back to France, and Scroby had gone too. And the girl?

Miss Scroby sprang up and went to her writing table to write to Richard at the Lune d'Italie for an explanation. At the Lune d'Italie. She only knew he was there because she had employed a private detective to trace him, and that thought stopped her dead. Decent people did not employ detectives to spy into other people's private affairs. Certainly not. But she had done it.

"It's his own fault," she said, "he ought to have told me where he was. I was naturally anxious." She picked up the pen.

"My dear Richard, I have been so anxious that I employed a private detective—"

Oh no, impossible.

"You will never guess how I found out where you are. A private detective—"

Miss Scroby tore up both sheets into small pieces and read Mr. Perkins' letter again.

"If you wish any further enquiries to be made, I could send a man over to Paris."

She went across to the window and stared into the garden. There were still rings in the low branch of that beech where Richard's swing used to hang, and now he was in Paris with a girl in embroidered stockings.

She went to the telephone and rang up Messrs. Percival, Perkins and Pink.

A few days later a report reached her. Mr. Scroby was still at the Lune d'Italie. He had hired a car for occasional use and his manservant drove him about. There were two gentlemen named Latimer also staying at that hotel; it seemed that they were relations of Mr. Scroby's since they called him "Cousin." One at least was an American. She laid down the report.

"I remember," said Angela Scroby to herself. "Those impertinent boys who used to run in and out of old Mrs. Latimer's house at Richmond in Virginia. They were great-nephews or something, one was called Gary and the other—it doesn't matter. They put a nest of baby mice in my knitting bag; they were horrid boys. I had to be firm with Richard, I remember; he thought their tiresome tricks were so clever. So they have turned up in Paris, how irritating."

"But," said her common sense, "how preferable to a French baggage in nylons. Besides, they have probably grown out of practical jokes by now; they must be in their thirties."

She picked up the report and read on.

"Mr. Scroby has recently been seen in the company of a young lady, but as she is not staying at the Lune d'Italie no particulars are immediately available."

"I knew it!" said Miss Scroby, so fiercely that her common sense took fright and hid behind the piano. "I knew it! Now I *shall* go to Paris."

She folded up the report and locked it in her desk. She had never been in Paris in her life, and such French as she had learned at school had died of atrophy years before. She was a little daunted at the prospect of going there alone, but that would not stop her.

"Plenty of people go to Paris," she said, "the most extraordinary people. I mean, the most ordinary people. Miss Timmins went last year. I shall want a new passport. Where does one apply for passports?

"Miss Timmins went to the Louvre. I could go there.

"I need not go alone, I could take Millicent."

But at this suggestion her common sense rushed out from behind the piano and told her firmly that the idea was ridiculous. If it was nearly impossible to induce Richard to take a fancy to Millicent in England, it would be quite impossible in Paris. Millicent against a Paris background was practically unthinkable even to Miss Scroby. Millicent, she felt, would be at a disadvantage in Paris. No, not take Millicent.

"I shall go to Paris by myself," she said aloud.

The morning after the abortive attack upon Scroby, Jules and Fingers met in Fingers' room to lament the past and discuss the future so far as Fingers could be said to discuss anything. What happened was that Jules talked and Fingers decided.

"What happened to you?" asked Jules. "You was in that archway, wasn't you? I saw you. But when I was in trouble you wasn't there."

Fingers, who looked even more pallid than usual and appeared to have a headache, merely glowered and made no answer.

"You look pretty sick," said Jules, "but it was me that had the worst of the deal." He detailed the story of his hair-raising drive round Paris. "And when I turned to tell the driver to be a bit more careful, there wasn't one. The driving-seat was empty, I tell you, at least that's what I thought. But of course I know now; I was thinking it over in bed last night. There was someone in the back with Scroby, slipped in when I wasn't looking and sat on the floor. Then, when he jumped out when I stopped, this man rose up behind and drugged me. You know how you feel when you've had a shot in hospital? Sort of vague and swimmy and you see some things and not others, and bright lights whirling and noises in your head? Like that. Of course if I'd realized what had been done to me—"

"No," said Fingers.

"No? What d'you mean, no?"

"I told you," said Fingers slowly, "to let those two alone."

"What two? You told us that you'd got the wind up over Scroby's two friends—"

Fingers nodded and then winced as though the movement hurt him.

"But they weren't there," said Jules, staring.

"They were."

"But, Fingers—what d'you mean—did you see them? When?"

"When I was hit," said Fingers, and took his head in his hands.

"You were stunned."

"Not then. And you weren't drugged."

"You're ill," said Jules in a tone of concern. "You've had concussion. You should stay in bed. What, arc you trying to tell me that what took me for a drive round Paris was Scroby's two friends and I couldn't see them?"

"That's right."

Jules made a rude noise expressing incredulity, and added: "Why couldn't I see them?"

"Think it over."

Jules shook his head slowly and there was a long pause broken, for a wonder, by Fingers.

"No more Scroby," he said.

"Oh, all right, if you say so. It's true we don't seem to have much luck with him, somehow. I suppose Pépi's gone for good, has he? Scared off, too?"

"He's gone," said Fingers.

"Not much loss. Soft, that's Pépi. What do we do now?"

"Marseilles."

"You like walking?" said Jules, and laughed harshly. "We have not even the money for the fare."

Fingers looked faintly amused and pointed at Jules' wristwatch.

"Oh no, we don't," said Jules firmly. "I tell you, no. I do not part with it, I prefer to walk."

Fingers almost smiled, for Jules' wristwatch was his most treasured— indeed, his only treasured—possession. It was a very good watch; it had a perfectly plain stainless steel case but it was, like the King's Daughter, all glorious within, for it had been made by Longines. Its previous owner was untimely dead, but Jules always thought of him with pleasure. He had unintentionally provided the watch.

"I tell you what," said Jules. "We stay here a week. We work hard, we make all the money we can in a week, and then we skip. Eh?"

"That's right," said Fingers.

There was an open-air meeting the following evening in the Place de la Bastille. It was either a Communist meeting to ginger up the Socialists or a Socialist meeting to discredit the Communists; it does not matter and Fingers did not care. The point was that there would be several hundred people there, moving about, jostling each other, and having their attention distracted by impassioned speakers. They would not, of course, be rich people in that crowd, but it is obvious that if one collects enough wallets the sum total of their contents may be very satisfactory indeed.

Fingers said that he would have Jules with him and Jules should wear his big overcoat with the deep pockets. As fast as Fingers collected wallets he would pass them to Jules; thus, if any misfortune happened and Fingers were accused of picking pockets, he could be searched without any evidence of guilt being found. No one would ever suspect Jules of picking pockets—he was manifestly incapable of anything so delicately skillful—but as regards the money, Fingers knew he could trust him. It should not take long, half an hour or so. The idea was to work quickly and get away before people discovered that they had been robbed.

"We had better meet in a café somewhere," said Jules, "empty the wallets, and get rid of them on the way home. We don't want a lot of recognizable rubbish on these premises."

"Tangier Jacques'," suggested Fingers, and Jules nodded. Tangier Jacques did not poke his nose into what did not concern him.

The scheme went off according to plan and without a hitch; Fingers collected some thirty-odd wallets which he slid into Jules' pockets while Jules himself did nothing but shift slowly about from place to place and stare open-mouthed at the fiery-tongued orators who addressed him. The only faintly disappointing aspect was that so many of the victims realized their losses almost at once, since it is a fact that the less money you have the more care you take of it.

Even the fiery-tongued orators noticed that their indignation meeting was not the only one being held on the Place de la Bastille that evening; there was another upon the edge of the crowd which was centered about a gendarme. He, poor man, was receiving complaints.

"I have been robbed!"

"All my money—it is gone!"

"What do we pay the police for? They stand about looking silly while we, the hard-working ones, are robbed under their noses."

"I have been robbed!"

"Arrest the thief!"

"My wallet—"

Fingers nudged Jules and moved away. Jules drifted after him and they went together to the café run by Tangier Jacques. This is a dark smoky place just off the Rue de Lappe; there is a front room containing a bar and a few marble-topped tables; through an archway at the back there is another room just as smoky and grubby as the front room and even darker since it has no window to the outer air at all and precious little outer air either. The lights are dim and badly placed; this is intentional, for the convenience of those who frequent it. They are not genuinely shy but they do shun observation. There are also three or four small alcoves; these are more private still. Fingers led the way to one of these and Jules followed him. The bartender's assistant, a beefy young man with a striped jersey and crew-cut hair, came to take their order.

"A little glass—" began Fingers.

"Little glass be hanged," said Jules, squashing himself and his large overcoat into a chair at the back of the alcove. "I say, a bottle of champagne."

"*Bien, m'sieu,*" said the man, and looked at Fingers for confirmation, but Fingers only nodded, so the man went away.

"We're celebrating, aren't we?" said Jules obstinately, though he kept his voice low. "Know how many there were? Thirty-seven, that's what. Thirty-seven."

Fingers nodded.

"And today's payday," exulted Jules. "What we've got here"—he dropped his voice even lower—"will take us South in comfort and keep us for a while when we get there. We can go tomorrow if we like and then maybe you will stop seeing bogies everywhere you look and act reasonable again. Sunshine," said Jules lyrically, "sunshine in your bones is what you want."

The large young man came with a bottle of champagne and two glasses. There was, indeed, no silly nonsense about an ice pail, but he did make a little ceremony about extracting the cork, which flew out and hit the ceiling. The wine was poured with a flourish, the bottle was set down on the table, and the young man grinned at them and left them to it.

"There's something about champagne," said Jules, and enlarged upon the subject between sips. He also spoke of the blue Mediterranean, the fish-stalls in the Marseilles markets, the wine in the Marseilles *bistros*, and a girl he used to know in the Cannebiere. He told a funny story about her, but Fingers did not laugh, nor had he said anything whatever since they sat down, though once he shivered suddenly. But Jules took no notice, he was used to Fingers' silences.

Presently the bottle was empty; also, a group of three men and a woman, who had been sitting at the other side of the room, got up and went out.

Fingers, who had been waiting for them to go, stretched out his hand across the table and said: "One by one."

Jules leaned back from the table and tried to push his hands into his coat pockets, but the space was constricted and his big coat was bunched round him.

"My pockets are so full," he said happily, "that I can't get my hands in." He stood up, shook his coat straight, and tried again. This time his hands went in easily—too easily.

He snatched them out and plunged them in again and his eyes widened until the white showed all round the dark irises. He felt frantically in all the corners as though thirty-seven wallets had shrunk together to the size of a crumpled tram ticket which a man might fail to find, and his sallow face turned a greenish yellow in the discolored light.

He threw his coat open and felt in the inside pockets and in those of his suit, and his breath came in gasps as though he had been running. The large young man in the striped jersey, seeing one of his customers standing up as preparing to leave, came across to be paid for the champagne. At this, Jules' powers of speech returned to him and he let out a howl of anguish which made everyone look round.

"I've been robbed! *Sacré*—! I've been robbed!"

Fingers sat there as though turned to stone; even his eyelids did not move and his hands were stiff and still.

"Four hundred and fifty francs, messieurs," said the young man, referring to the champagne.

"But I've been robbed," said Jules, turning an agonized face upon the waiter. "Every penny I had! My own, too."

"I regret," said the young man, and turned enquiring eyes upon Fingers, who blinked and moved and felt in his own pockets, though as one without hope.

"I also," he said, and let his empty hands fall slackly upon the table.

But the broad-shouldered waiter with the crew cut was not easily impressed and had heard tales like this before.

"When one orders champagne," he said, "and drinks it all up"—he tilted the empty bottle—"one also pays for it, *mes gars.* Make no mistake." He retained the bottle in one hand in case the massive Jules should give trouble, but Jules was not feeling energetic at all. "I speak to the proprietor," continued the waiter, "and we call the police, yes?"

"No," said Jules, and sat down with a bump. Fingers, who was staring at the floor, glanced up at him for a moment and then down again.

"I do not wish to appear disobliging," said the young man civilly. "Monsieur"—he addressed Jules—"is wearing what appears to be an excellent wristwatch. If he would care to deposit it with the proprietor, the greatest care will be taken of it and it can, naturally, be redeemed at any time."

Jules made an odd humming sound through his nose—it sounded like an exasperated wasp on a windowpane—but Fingers laid both hands on the table and rose to his feet with a jerk.

"Give it," he said.

Jules, with shaking fingers, slowly unbuckled the strap and drew his adored Longines from his wrist.

CHAPTER XII
Miss Scroby

IN THE MEANTIME the Station Sergeant at the nearest Quartier police station was drowsing behind his desk. Things were quiet at the moment and would probably remain so for as long as that open-air meeting lasted; if it ended in uproar he would be busy half the night taking statements and issuing orders. But so long as things remained quiet it was permissible to relax for a moment. He put his elbows on his desk, propped his head in both hands, and closed his eyes.

He was disturbed less than a minute later by the sound of something slipping on his desk. Something soft; if the office had not for once been so quiet he would not have heard it. He thought about it for a moment and then raised his head and looked round.

In the square tray labelled IN, which had been empty when the Sergeant closed his eyes, there was a pile of wallets. Black, brown, and blue wallets, cheap new ones and cheap shabby ones and even a few which, though old and battered now, had once been expensive and good, notably one of crocodile leather with silver corners, one missing. The wallets had simply been deposited in the tray in an untidy heap and the top ones were still slipping. Even as the Sergeant stared with bolting eyes, one insecurely poised wallet slid from the top of the pile and missed the rim of the tray to fall with a very faint thump upon the desk itself. Within six inches of the Sergeant's right elbow, in fact. He withdrew the elbow sharply.

After a moment he rubbed his eyes, gave himself a sharp pinch on the thigh, stood up to stamp his feet as though they were cold, and then sat down again. The wallets were still there.

Five minutes later there was the sound of trampling feet and excited voices in the street outside; the door opened and a gendarme walked in, the same who had been the recipient of hard luck stories in the Place de la Bastille a little earlier. He walked up to the desk and saluted, and behind him the office filled with the indignant persons of thirty-seven bereaved citizens of Paris.

"*Mon Sergent,*" said the gendarme, "there has been an outbreak of pocket-picking in the crowd attending that meeting. Thirty-seven citizens have complained and I brought them along here for convenience in taking down so many names and addresses and particulars of losses." His eyes fell upon the pile of wallets which even now the Sergeant had not prevailed upon himself to touch. The gendarme gasped and fell silent.

Not so the bereaved ones, for they pressed forward and laid their complaints in loud voices, all speaking at once and employing a wealth of gesture to emphasize their distress. Nor did they confine their remarks to their names, addresses, and statements of loss; they added in a roar of picturesque if uncultured imagery their opinion of Paris police in general and of those of this Quartier in particular. The faces, the personal habits, the attention to duty, the intelligence and even the honesty of the police came under most unfavorable review until at last a tall thin man in the front row tired of shouting into the Sergeant's ox-like face and happened to glance at the pile of wallets instead. Instantly he stiffened, let out a yell which drowned the rest, and shot out a pointing finger.

"That crocodile-skin one with the missing corner! That is mine!"

The Sergeant picked it up and asked for the name and address and description of contents, and the office fell into silence to hear the answer. There was a name inside, it was so-and-so, there was about so much money, a half-used book of Metro tickets, a National Lottery ticket of which the last numbers were 234, and two postage stamps.

"Correct," said the Sergeant. "Dupont, make out a receipt and Monsieur will sign it. Next, please."

This, of course, was bluff, since the Sergeant had no means of knowing that these wallets belonged to those people, but one certainly did and he gambled on the rest. In the end and after a certain amount of argument over uncertainties, thirty-seven wallets were claimed and there remained two in the tray.

"Now," said the Sergeant, pushing his glasses up on his forehead and glowering under them at the assembly, "now I shall be glad to learn whether the company sees any reason to modify its opinion that the police force is staffed exclusively by the moronic and morally unreliable products of orphanages for the children of mentally deficient parents with criminal records. Don't all speak at once."

Most of them murmured some kind of apology and a few were downright flattering.

"That's quite nice," said the Sergeant. "Very nice of you indeed, but don't sound so damned surprised about it. All signed receipts? Magnificent. Good evening, the company."

The company filed out and left the Sergeant and the gendarme looking at each other.

"These two remaining," said the gendarme, "will presumably be claimed later."

"Presumably," agreed the Sergeant, and opened them both. "No names. No addresses. No stamps. No lottery tickets. And precious little money. You may resume your duty, Dupont."

"Certainly, *mon Sergent.* But—"

"But what?"

"But, may I ask, how did they come here? The wallets, I mean, it was so quick. I mean, all of them. I mean—"

"I am sure you do," said the Sergeant smoothly, "but, Dupont if I told you, you would not understand. Resume your patrol, Dupont."

"Very good, *mon Sergent.*"

Dupont went out and the Sergeant sat still, looking at the two shabby wallets left on his desk. Eventually he got to his feet, shook his head impatiently, and locked up the wallets in the office safe.

"Heaven knows," he said aloud, and added, "presumably."

Pépi not only broke off relations with Fingers Dupré and Jules, he also packed up all his possessions, mainly clothes, and moved to a different lodging in quite another part of Paris, nor did he leave a forwarding address behind him. He had a little money of his own, not enough to live on but enough to keep him, with care and economy, between periods of employment. He therefore went out to look for another period of employment; that is, a trusting stranger.

Strangers arrive at railway stations; travelers from London in particular arrive at the Gare du Nord. Since Pépi could speak very fair English he used to drop in at the Gare du Nord to look for what he called a prospect.

One evening, just when the famous Flèche d'Or had glided to an imperceptible stop, Pépi strolled along the platform with exactly the air of one who has come on the chance of meeting a friend who might possibly be there. He was not fussed and anxious but mildly enquiring and very ready to be pleased. He made his way slowly among the alighting passengers, glancing up at the train windows as he went.

The Flèche d'Or is a Pullman train with the doors at either end of each coach and there are steep and rather awkward steps down to ground level. At the head of one of these, the Chef du Train was calling to one of the travelers.

"Mademoiselle! Mademoiselle Scroby! Here is your small case—can you manage—"

"Oh, thank you. So kind. Yes, I can manage perfectly."

The name of Scroby stopped Pépi in his tracks. Of course there might be no connection—Scroby might be a common name in England for all he knew—but he could not help being interested. There was a little more talk within the carriage. "No, that is all, thank you. My large case is among the registered baggage." A momentary pause in which presumably money changed hands since the Chef du Train was being audibly grateful, and then a lady came down the steps.

She was gray-haired, very neat, and eminently respectable. She wore a severely plain gray coat and skirt and a small black hat. She was a little impeded in descending the steps because she was carrying an attaché case, a handbag, a sort of shopping bag with loop handles over her arm, and an umbrella. She hesitated at the last long step down and Pépi sprang forward to put a respectful hand under one elbow to steady her. The other hand swept off his hat.

"Excuse, please—allow me. These steps, they are dangerous."

She stepped down and then turned to look at him with very keen gray eyes under severely straight brows. Pépi thought her a little alarming and was preparing to back away when suddenly she smiled, and the smile was unexpectedly pleasant.

"Thank you," she said, "that was thoughtful of you."

"Enchanted, madame," he said, and bowed.

She nodded kindly, moved a step or two forward, and looked rather vaguely about her. By this time most of the passengers had hurried on and the platform was clearing.

"Could I, perhaps, direct Madame?"

"Perhaps you know where one goes to claim the registered baggage, do you?"

"But certainly, this way. May I," suggested Pépi deferentially, "be permitted to escort Madame?"

Another straight glance from those penetrating gray eyes; Pépi sustained it with an effort.

"That's very good of you, young man, but am I not keeping you?"

"Oh no, madame," he said, falling into step beside her. "I came here to meet a friend, but he is not arrived. May I carry some—"

"No, thank you, I have all my things together and they are not heavy. Where is this place? Along here? What a huge station this is."

"But noisy, madame. Excuse me," and he steered her gently out of the path of a dashing porter with a loaded barrow. "It is the first time Madame has come to the Gare du Nord?"

"Not only that, it is my first visit to Paris. It—I find it quite exciting."

She smiled at him again.

"I hope that Madame will be very happy here. This way, madame, in here for the Customs. May I be allowed to come with?"

"I suppose," she said doubtfully, "they all speak English? I have forgotten all the French I ever learned."

"*Allons*," said Pépi cheerfully, and urged her in. The simple formalities were soon done and the suitcase handed over.

"And now," he said, "a taxi?"

"Yes, please. But first, a porter to carry this."

"What is the matter with me?" he asked, laughing. "I have two arms, madame, with hands attached, reasonably strong, thank God." He picked up the suitcase. "This way, madame."

She walked briskly beside him out of the Customs shed into the court-yard where the taxis wait in droves. One of them drew up and Pépi put the suitcase inside.

"Where shall I tell the man to go?"

To his surprise, she hesitated.

"I don't know—some quiet hotel."

"Madame has not booked?"

"No. No, I haven't. A nephew of mine is at the Lune d'Italie, but I don't want to stay in the same one. I prefer to be completely independent."

Pépi believed that at once; Miss Scroby—he had checked her name on the luggage labels—was nothing if not completely independent. And she was that Scroby's aunt. Most interesting.

"May I suggest? My own hotel where I go when I am at Paris, it is quiet and good. Not too expensive." He smiled confidentially. "If Madame would care to see?"

"Yes. Yes, I will see it, if it is not too far out. Are you staying there now?"

"Since my friend is not come, I think so, yes. It is called the Couronne de Navarre—the Crown of Navarre, you know?"

"Henry the Fourth. I read Dumas when I was young. Shall we go together, then, if it suits you?"

"Admirable, madame." He handed her into the taxi, told the man where to go, and asked Miss Scroby's permission to sit beside her. Since the Hôtel de la Couronne de Navarre is in the street called the Chaussée d'Antin, the drive was not a long one and the taxi stopped at a recessed entrance between two shops. Pépi took out the luggage, Miss Scroby paid off the taxi, waving Pépi away, and together they walked towards the flight of steps which led up to the door.

"Not a very imposing entrance, madame," said Pépi apologetically. "The hotel is all upstairs, over these shops."

"I have no particular use," said Miss Scroby briskly, "for an imposing entrance, especially as no doubt the cost of it would be included in the bill. There is no sense in paying for nonessentials."

"*Bien sûr,* madame," said Pépi who was, in fact, a little outpaced by this incursion into practical economics. He held open the swing door and she preceded him into the narrow entrance hall with the porter's desk at the end, beyond the stairs. Pépi put down the luggage and walked up to the desk to greet the porter.

"Good evening," he said in English. "I am here again, as you see." The man smiled an apology and answered in French in a friendly manner, since no hotel porter will ever admit that he does not recognize a guest.

"I am sorry, madame," said Pépi, "this man does not speak English—"

"Onlee two—three words," put in the porter.

"Perhaps I can say for you what you want?"

Miss Scroby would be grateful. A single room, not too high up, and so forth, and she would like to see it before booking in. The porter sized her up with an unerring eye; the good luggage, the well-cut suit, the expensive handbag, the small diamond earrings, and dashed out to display his domain. The *salle à manger* on the left, the salon on the right. "Lounge, yes? Oui, madame," and Pépi hovered in the background with a benign smile. The porter believed he might have a room vacant and conducted the usual frenzied search through the register. Hall porters will conduct a frenzied search if there is not a single guest in the place; it looks well. Yes, one upon the first floor, Madame would like to see it? But, naturally. He rang a bell; a chambermaid appeared and took Miss Scroby upstairs.

Pépi and the porter smiled at each other.

"And now, for me," said Pépi. "A small room?"

"Also first floor, monsieur?"

"Good gracious, no. Far too expensive. One must make the economies in these days."

"Alas, yes, who must not?" sighed the porter, and offered him a room on the third floor. Pépi was still considering it when Miss Scroby came down the stairs.

"Very nice," she said. "Do perfectly well." She nodded at the porter, who beamed at her, produced the little form which travelers must fill up, and asked for her passport.

"What—oh, I see. Thank you, I see that this form is in English as well as French, so I can manage perfectly well." She withdrew to a corner of the desk.

"I'll take that room," said Pépi to the porter. "I will go and fetch my luggage, I left it at the station. I will book in when I come back." He approached Miss Scroby. "You will be all right now, yes? I have my usual room here, now I go to fetch my luggage. We meet, perhaps, later?"

"I hope so. Thank you very much for all your help."

"A pleasure, madame," said Pépi, and meant it. He turned to go, but she called him back.

"A moment, young man, what is your name?"

Pépi snatched out his wallet and gave her a card which she read aloud.

"Philippe Morand. Thank you, Mr. Morand."

She turned again to the tiresome little form; Pépi walked out and tittuped happily down the steps. A prospect, a definite prospect. A nice rich lady new to Paris and with apparently few friends except nephew Scroby. Something in her tone when she mentioned Scroby had suggested that she was not very pleased with him. It should be possible to avoid Scroby. Pépi reproached himself with only one slip; he had given Miss Scroby one of his own cards instead of selecting a more aristocratic name from the collection he carried about with him. The Comte de Somewhere would have sounded better. Never mind. He went back to his own lodgings and packed a good-looking suitcase.

Hawkes, the journalist who had taken Richard Scroby to the séance, returned to Paris after a fortnight's absence upon various assignments. He was glad to be back; Paris was where he lived. He spent the first evening tucking himself comfortably into his own tiny flat with his own things about him and let his mind run over the various matters which had engaged him before he went away. One of them was Scroby, incredulously awaiting the onset of a brace of ancestral ghosts. Probably Scroby had returned to London already, but it was just worth asking. Hawkes rang up the Hôtel de la Lune d'Italie. Was Mr. Richard Scroby still in residence there?

"But, yes, monsieur," said the hall porter. "We are happy in the continued presence of Monsieur Scroby. He is not, however, in the hotel this evening; he gave me to understand that he was going to the theater."

"Oh, thank you. It doesn't matter."

"And Monsieur's name?"

"Never mind. I'll ring him, or come round."

"*Bien,* monsieur."

Hawkes found himself in the neighborhood of the Rue Caumartin the following morning, so he went into the Lune d'Italie. The porter was not sure whether Monsieur Scroby was in or not, should he ring up to the room?

"Don't trouble," said Hawkes, and galloped up the stairs two at a time. Wilkins would know all about the ghosts and, besides, Hawkes had a piece of news for Scroby. He knocked at the door and Wilkins admitted him.

"I regret, sir, that Mr. Scroby is out, but I expect him in at any moment. Would you care to come in, sir? Mr. Scroby was saying only yesterday that he had not had the pleasure of seeing you lately, sir."

"No, I've been away on business, only got back last night."

"No doubt, sir, that would account for it. Would you care to take a little something, sir—a glass of sherry, possibly?"

"Yes, please. I was mildly surprised to find you were still here. I imagine all the excitement about Mr. Scroby's burglar has died down long ago."

"I presume so, sir," said Wilkins, filling a sherry glass to exactly the right level. "We receive the English papers regularly and, apart from a short intimation that the man has been committed for trial at the Central Criminal Court on the capital charge, there has been no further mention of the affair. A cigarette, sir? Or would you prefer a cigar?"

"Cigarette, thanks. Your master must be enjoying Paris, since he is prolonging his stay. Not that a fortnight or so is a long visit."

"But outlasting the emergency, sir."

"Precisely. Wilkins, you ought to have my job."

"Writing for the Press, sir?"

"That's right. You have an unerring choice of words."

"Thank you, sir. I may say that I have sometimes considered journalism as a career but have always decided against engaging in it."

"Why, Wilkins?"

Wilkins shifted his weight from one foot to the other.

"If I may say so, sir, and without the faintest intention of giving even the smallest degree of offense—"

"Go on."

"A rackety life, sir. I have not, I feel, the figure for it."

Hawkes ran his eye over Wilkins' sedate but ample curves and grinned suddenly.

"You may be right. But, tell me, what does your master find to amuse him in Paris? He can't chase snuffboxes all day."

"Er—no, sir."

"Wilkins, you are amused. There is a twinkle in your eye. You don't mean that he's found a lady?"

"I could not, sir, permit myself for a moment the indiscretion of discussing my master's affairs—"

"Not even with a boyhood friend?"

"Not at all, sir."

"I respect your scruples, Wilkins. But—by Jove—I wonder if that accounts for it."

Wilkins turned suddenly to open the door and Scroby walked in.

CHAPTER XIII
They Only Fade .Away

SCROBY seemed a little subdued, not unhappy but a trifle absent, as though some part of his thoughts was far away. He greeted Hawkes with pleasure and said that he was sorry to have kept him waiting. "A friend of mine," he said, with the ingenuous frankness of one whose topmost thoughts must bubble out. "We spent the morning together because they are going to Chartres this afternoon."

"They?"

"She and her mother." Scroby looked at his watch. "The train goes just after one; she didn't leave herself much time."

"Do I gather," said Hawkes with interest, "that I have to congratulate you?"

"What? Oh well, it's not fixed up yet or anything like it, but I do seem to be changing my mind a bit on the subject of marriage. The really important thing," said Scroby earnestly, "is to pick the right one. Not bossy, you know."

"So you haven't announced it yet?"

"Great heavens, no, I haven't asked her yet. One can't rush these things, you know; besides, why should one?"

"And your aunt Angela—" began Hawkes.

"Of course I shall have to tell her when it's all fixed up, but I'll have everything cut and dried and the wedding day fixed before I—What's the matter?"

"I assumed she knew."

"Knew? How the devil could she know? She doesn't even know that I'm in Paris. 'Assumed she knew'—why?"

"I supposed that that was why she had come to Paris."

Scroby staggered.

"*What?*"

"I saw her this morning, strolling round the Galeries Lafayette. I'd gone in to buy myself a tie, and—"

"Hawkes, I'm sorry, but you're raving. Aunt Angela can't be in Paris. She doesn't care for traveling, she can't speak French, and she despises foreigners. You were mistaken, you saw someone like her; it's ages since you last met—"

"No, it isn't," said Hawkes. "She and you and I had lunch together at Scott's just before I went to Quebec last year for—"

"Oh, lord, of course we did."

"Besides, I've known her for years, you know that. She used to take us out when we were at school. It's you that's raving, Scroby."

"Did you speak to her this morning?"

"Well, no, I didn't. I rather gathered from you—well, anyway, I dodged round one of those big stands they hang ties on, you know, and when I peered round again she was walking up the stairs. Perhaps she's only just arrived. Is she going to stay here, do you know?"

Scroby leapt as though someone had stuck a pin into him.

"I don't know at all, but I do know I'm not." He snatched up his coat, dashed into his bedroom, and returned pushing his passport and a folder of traveler's checks into his pocket. "Excuse my dashing off like this, Hawkes, I've got a train to catch. I shall do it with luck. Wilkins, I'm going to Chartres. Pack some things and bring the car down tomorrow. Keep these rooms on. Good-bye, I'm off."

"But, sir," said Wilkins in an agonized tone, "at least a toothbrush and pajamas—"

"Buy those at Chartres," said Scroby, going out the door.

"Sir, sir, to what hotel—"

"The Grand Monarque."

Flying footsteps down the passage; the outer door slammed and Wilkins came back into the sitting room.

"Young blood, sir," he said indulgently. "Young blood."

"Who is the lady?" asked Hawkes, fiddling with the strap of his wrist-watch.

"A Miss Virginia Townsend from Charlottesville in the United States of America, sir. A very charming young lady. She is in Paris with her mother, studying antiques, I understand."

"You approve of this prospect, do you, Wilkins?"

"Certainly, sir. A little more sherry—allow me. I should retain my situation under the altered circumstances; my master and I have already gone into the question."

"And you have really heard nothing of Miss Scroby being in Paris?"

"Not a word, sir. Excuse me, sir, did I understand that there was not the slightest possibility of a mistake in identity?"

"Not a hope, Wilkins. I practically met her face to face, but she was looking the other way. By the time she turned her head I was tying up my shoelace and the moment she passed I nipped behind one of those revolving stands. You see, I wasn't clear how much Mr. Scroby had told her and I didn't want to release shoals of cats from a whole pile of bags."

"Precisely, sir. Most awkward, if I may say so."

"Excellent sherry, this."

"I am glad that it is to your taste, sir. The range and variety in sherries is so great that, to suit every taste, one should have a comprehensive cellar of that wine alone. The prospect of being able, from the ordinarily limited selection in private households, to suit the taste of any one visitor is, therefore, largely fortuitous."

"No doubt. Oh yes, there was something else I meant to ask your master—in fact, that was one reason why I came in this morning—what happened about the ghosts?"

"Ghosts, sir?"

"Have you forgotten? The message from two ghosts at that séance we went to. I know you heard all about it; we were telling you about it that same evening after we got back and you told us about seeing an earlier Lord Welter with his head under his arm."

"I remember, sir. He presented a most curious appearance."

"These ghosts said that they were going to come along if I remember correctly. What were their names, now—Latimer, that was it."

"There are two gentlemen named Latimer, sir, staying in this hotel at the moment. Mr. Scroby gave me to understand that they were cousins of his. Very nice gentlemen, sir. We see a good deal of them. They are out today. I understand that they have gone to the races at Longchamp, sir."

"Oh, indeed," said Hawkes, losing interest. "An odd coincidence, that. I must get on, Wilkins. You go to Chartres tomorrow, do you?"

"Tomorrow afternoon, sir, I anticipate leaving for Chartres. There are one or two small matters to attend to in the morning."

"I hope you have a good run," said Hawkes, and went about his business.

That night when he went to bed he felt in his pockets for his wrist-watch, but it was not to be found. The strap had broken when he was in Scroby's room that morning and he would have sworn he put the watch in his pocket, intending to get a new strap fitted in the afternoon, but he had been busy and forgotten about it. He was annoyed; it was a good watch and he valued it. It was just possible he had left it in Scroby's room; it was worth asking. He rang up the hotel in the morning, but Wilkins had gone out. It would be necessary to get in touch with him before he left for Chartres; Hawkes went to the Lune d'Italie about midday and was told that Wilkins was there.

Hawkes went up and found Wilkins relieved to see him; the watch had been found in the seat of his chair.

"Please come in, sir," said Wilkins, holding the door open. "I was a little perturbed, sir, not knowing how to get in touch with you and thinking you might be anxious. I have it here, sir."

"Thank you so much," said Hawkes, following along the short passage. "Careless of me, I've had it for years and don't want to lose it. Oh—er—good morning."

There were two tall men standing by the table and talking in low tones together; they turned when he came in.

"Good morning, sir," said the elder of the two. "Are you also seeking our fugitive cousin Scroby? It seems that he has fled to Chartres."

"I knew that he'd gone," said Hawkes; "in fact, I was here yesterday when he fled, which is, believe me, exactly the right word. No, I came today in the hope that Wilkins might have found my watch, and here it is. Thank you, Wilkins, I am most grateful."

"Then you must be Mr. Hawkes, for Wilkins was telling us about the watch. Our name is Latimer, Mr. Hawkes."

"Scroby's cousins," said Hawkes, shaking hands.

"This certainly is a pleasure, Mr. Hawkes," said Charles. "We saw you at that séance but it was not possible to make ourselves known to you then."

Hawkes grinned appreciatively, for he thought he understood. These two were at the séance, had seen Scroby come in, and, all on the spur of the moment, had worked off a family joke upon him. Excellent people.

"Of course not," he said. "I quite understand."

"Without doubt Richard told you about us," said James. "Now his sudden departure has left us in something of a difficulty."

Hawkes jumped to his second wrong conclusion within a minute; he thought that they had lost money at the races yesterday. Hawkes himself was not at all well off; it would be more tactful to change the subject.

"Tiresome blighter," he said vaguely. "By the way, since you are his relations I take it that you know why he went off like that?"

"Wilkins told us that Richard's aunt Angela has appeared in Paris," said Charles. "I reckon that that excellent lady has him scared stiff. Yes, sir, I opine that she terrifies him."

"I gather that she is deeply attached to him," said James, "and has nurtured him from earliest childhood. He must feel that he owes her a great deal."

"Oh, he does," said Hawkes, "but she shouldn't treat him as though he were still at his prep school, you know. It isn't fair. However, on this occasion he wasn't sorry to have an excuse to dash off to Chartres. I expect you know all about that, too."

"Sir," said James delightedly, "we introduced them."

Wilkins came in and asked if the gentlemen would like a little something and they thought it a good idea.

"And a small glass of red wine of some kind, if we may," said Charles, "you know."

"Certainly, sir," said Wilkins. "With pleasure."

He came back with a tray of decanters and glasses and one glass filled with claret. Hawkes wondered why, possibly some medicinal requirement which was no concern of his. The red wine was set in the middle of the table and Wilkins began pouring sherry while Charles idly snapped his fingers as a man does when he is trying to remember something.

Hawkes turned aside to take a cigarette from a box and light it; as he turned back to the table he saw something which, for a passing second, he took to be a wisp of smoke from an ashtray. But it was not; it was too big, it was too transparent, it had a definite shape, it rounded and solidified by rapid degrees, it was a small brown monkey in a little red jacket and cap. What was so particularly shocking was that no one except himself seemed to find anything odd about it. The taller Latimer stretched out a long finger to rub the creature behind the ear and it tilted its head like a cat. Wilkins moved the wineglass towards it with a smile and said: "There you are. Is that all right?"

Hawkes, who had been holding his breath, gasped and gasped again as though he had fallen into a tank of ice water. It seemed that he could not get his breath. James Latimer turned suddenly with an expression of concern.

"My dear Mr. Hawkes! Are you ill—what is it?"

Hawkes, quite beyond speech, pointed a shaking finger at the monkey, who took off its little cap and made him a polite bow.

Charles came round the table with long strides and threw one arm round Hawkes' shoulders. "It is only Ulysses; what upsets you so? That is my monkey; did Richard not tell you?"

"But," gasped Hawkes, "but he is a ghost."

"Of course he is, the Prussians shot him in 1870. I am right sorry, Mr. Hawkes, truly I am. But you did not appear to mind us; it never entered my mind that Ulysses would shock you so. Sit down, I beg. Wilkins!"

But Wilkins was already returning with a small glass of cognac.

"Drink this, sir, and try to breathe deeply and evenly."

"It's the darnedest thing," said Charles, straightening up as the color returned to Hawkes' face. "My cousin James and I can come and go as we please and no one is troubled, but when my poor Ulysses appears he mows down all before him. It reminds me of the Battle of Richmond. Yes, sir."

"Pray, Mr. Hawkes," said James, "are you sure you are quite recovered? Sir, it was prodigious thoughtless of us, we do most sincerely apologize. But, sir, when we mentioned the séance you said that you perfectly understood."

Hawkes blinked. "Please don't apologize, it was I who was slow on the uptake—do I really understand that you are both ghosts also?"

"That is certainly so, yes, sir. You do not object to our company, I hope? No qualms, no cold shivers down the spine? Mr. Hawkes, sooner than discommode you, we will go to our rooms at once; we did but come here to speak with Wilkins on a certain matter."

Hawkes was rapidly recovering; even before his pulse had regained its usual even tenor his newshound's instinct was awake and barking. This was a Story—and what a story!

Even while he disclaimed qualms and quivers of any kind his mind was arranging and amending phrases and laying out headlines.

"Nonsense, not at all," he said. "Nothing of the sort. Can't think what came over me—touch of liver or something. Look, if you want to talk to Wilkins I'll get along; we shall meet again soon, shan't we? Come and dine with me—what about tonight?"

"Mr. Hawkes, you are amazing kind and we shall be delighted," said James, "to accept your kind invitation in a few days' time, but at the moment we are much concerned to ask Wilkins if he will be so good as to convey us to Chartres. Our young cousin's abrupt departure has left us in an awkward predicament."

"Oh," said Hawkes, determined at all costs not to lose touch with his

Story, "do forgive me, but if it's only a question of—er—a temporary embarrassment till that blighter Scroby shows up again, couldn't I—"

Charles' dark face lit up with laughter. "Mr. Hawkes, you are a sportsman, yes, sir, and if it were only a question of money I should not hesitate to lean upon your generosity, but—"

"Let me explain," said James. "Mr. Hawkes, in our condition it is necessary for us to be in practically continual touch with someone of our own blood and lineage to have the power to appear solid and active as you see us now. For there is a continuing unity in a family which is, indeed, an entity in itself of which each member is an integral part. Members of families may disagree and quarrel and even part, Mr. Hawkes, but there remains the *Abstammunggeistblutheit* as the Germans call it, the Family-Spirit-Blood, which cannot be done away by any act of will. This it is, Mr. Hawkes, which maintains us in strength and energy and only Richard Scroby is available to supply it."

"Then what happens if—" began Hawkes.

"If we are parted from him? We wilt, Mr. Hawkes," said Charles. "We become languid, sir, which is bad enough, but, sir, the next stage is worse. We become gradually translucent at the extremities like soft and faintly pinkish glass; we shimmer like moonlight on summer lawns, yes, sir. We should finally disappear from mortal sight, leaving only our clothes to be seen walking about. A horrid sight."

Hawkes agreed. "It would be."

"We have been rash," said James. "Prompted by motives of delicacy and courtesy, we have absented ourselves from Richard's company to leave him free to pay his suit. Now, when we are beginning to be in urgent need of him, he has gone to Chartres. Wilkins, will you convey us thither?"

"Certainly, sir. Will it suit you to start at two-thirty?"

Charles held up a long thin hand in a ray of sunshine. Every human hand is partially translucent in a strong light, but Hawkes found himself reminded of Lalique glass.

"Make it two o'clock, Wilkins," said Charles.

"Very good, sir."

"I say," said Hawkes eagerly, "can I come along too? Just for the run, you know," he added unconvincingly. "It's such a lovely day and I can catch a train back. If you wouldn't mind."

"We should be more than delighted to have your company," said James. "A long drive on a fine day is, indeed, a pleasant experience."

"And then you can see what happens," said Charles with his slow wide smile. "Eh, Mr. Hawkes?"

Hawkes blushed faintly but stuck to his guns. When the car left the Lune d'Italie at two o'clock with Wilkins at the wheel, Hawkes was sitting beside him and the two Latimers, already a little shadowy, were in the rear seat together.

They talked to him as the car drove on and he turned in his seat, with his elbow on the back of it. James talked the most; Charles seemed content to sit back and idly watch the passing landscape as though he had not the energy to say much. They went through Versailles and James said that as a half-grown boy he had heard men talk who remembered the French Revolution. He drew some apposite morals upon the fallibility of human greatness. " 'The boast of heraldry, the pomp of power,' " he quoted. " 'The paths of glory,' Mr. Hawkes, 'lead but to the grave.' "

It is about sixty miles from Paris to Chartres; before they were half-way Hawkes began to wonder whether the Latimers would last the course. Their clothes and the hats which they did not remove were, of course, perfectly solid since their dematerialization was not a voluntary act, and Hawkes found a little disconcerting the way a hat would turn with the merest glimmer of a face under it, like a reflection dimly seen in a dusty window, or a coatsleeve would rise with but a hint of the gesturing hand beyond the speckless shirt cuff.

Charles sighed deeply and leaned back in his corner and James turned towards him with a suggestion of anxiety in his attitude.

"Wilkins," said James Latimer, "would it be possible to stop at some convenient café? It may be that a glass of wine would revive us."

"Certainly, sir. I will look out for one."

"There is quite a good roadhouse just round the next bend," said Hawkes. "It's a good place for a car to stop; there is a pull-in in front of it—there it is."

It was a cheerful place with gay striped curtains at the wide windows of a big room built out in front. Wilkins turned in and brought the car to a stop near the door. Hawkes asked what the Latimers would like, offering to go and fetch it, but they would not hear of any such thing.

"What, shall we go about to make a lackey out of you to serve our needs?" said James. "Certainly not, Mr. Hawkes, though it is prodigious civil of you to offer." Wilkins opened the door and the Latimers alighted. "Will you not join us, my dear sir?"

Hawkes, getting a good view of them in full sunlight, begged to be excused; he did not drink, he said, in the afternoon. Wilkins watched them cross to the entrance and then came back to his seat.

"Would you care to go and have a drink, Wilkins?"

"I think not, sir, if I may be permitted to decline." He started the engine again. "I think it perhaps advisable to keep the engine running, in case of any eventuality necessitating our—our getting to 'ell out of it—Blimey, look at that!"

The café was fairly full since the hour was a convenient one for a little something between lunch and dinner; the customers, sitting placidly at small tables about the room or on high stools at the bar, turned their heads to look at the two tall figures who had just alighted from the car outside. For a moment there was a dead silence as no one moved or breathed, but only for a moment—

The next minute Hawkes and Wilkins saw such of the windows as were not already open flung wide and the assembled company scrambling out of them. Young and old, men, women, and children stepped or climbed or fell over the low windowsills and fled in all directions; most of them to the cars parked in the forecourt, which were immediately started up and driven furiously away, but some merely ran round any adjacent corner and out of sight. The staff, recognizable in white linen jackets, emerged from a side door to scamper across the garden and away, followed closely by a stout man who seemed to be the proprietor. Last of all to leave the premises was a buxom woman in a tight black dress who trotted after the proprietor, calling, "Alphonse! Alphonse! Wait for me!" She could not run very fast because, clasped in her arms, she was carrying the cash register.

The sight of complete suits of clothes with no men inside is naturally unnerving.

Last of all, the Latimers came out. They climbed disconsolately back into the car, and Wilkins immediately drove off. There was a period of silence which Hawkes did not feel competent to break.

"My stars," said Charles eventually, "what dizzards we are, James!" He laughed uneasily.

"It is no laughing matter, Charles; we frightened those poor, decent undeserving people out of their seven senses and I am deeply abashed. You see, Mr. Hawkes, we have never been reduced to this extremity before, and though we had been warned of what would happen, I for one did not realize that it had actually taken place. To each other, we are still completely visible. Mr. Hawkes, I entreat you to tell us frankly, what do we look like?"

Hawkes gulped and said: "Nothing. I mean that literally. There are the clothes but nothing else. Major Latimer said that that was how it would be."

"I did," said Charles. "Yes, sir, I did, but what I did not realize was that we should not be aware of it. Sir, we are a pair of dunderpated loobies, how say you, Cousin James?"

James groaned in a deep and melancholy manner and added: "The sooner we are at Chartres, the better. Wilkins, my good man, could you not drive considerably faster?"

"With pleasure, sir," said Wilkins, and put his foot down.

CHAPTER XIV
Pépi's Prospect

THEY SWEPT down the long straight roads bordered, as is customary in France, with poplars. Fields, upholstered in different shades of green, were spread out upon either hand; the sun shone and the Latimers wound down the rear windows as though the fresh air were doing them good. They seemed disinclined to talk and Hawkes let them alone. It was impossible to be frightened of people so friendly and matter-of-fact about their state as were the Latimers, but there was undoubtedly something eerie about their appearance at the moment; besides, Hawkes was quite happy recasting his Story—Ghosts Are Real—and adding finishing touches to his turns of phrase. His fingers itched for his typewriter or even for a pencil and a sheet of paper.

Presently they passed, hardly slackening speed, down the long single street of a typical French main-road village. When England breaks out in what is daintily known as "ribbon development" there is a frightful fuss; letters are written to the papers, bylaws are passed by County Councils, and rightly. France takes a more practical view. If you build houses along a road which already exists, you are spared the expense of making and maintaining secondary roads. Let us by all means be spared expense.

At the far end of this village street a figure in a blue uniform saw the car approaching at a good forty-five miles an hour, for Wilkins had eased up a little. The blue figure stepped off the pavement into the road and held up his hand.

"He wants you to stop," said Hawkes, "that policeman."

"Yes, sir," said Wilkins, who knew that already, and he drew the car to a stop abreast of the Constable, who came forward, leaned one hand upon the ledge of the driver's window, and spoke to Wilkins. Did he not know that it was *absolument deféndu* to drive at some eighty kilometers

per hour through a village with a speed limit of thirty kilometers per hour?
Indefensible. Unpardonable. Disregarding the law. Contrary to the rules.
Selfishly unobservant of the safety of the public.

This stung James into action; before Hawkes could speak, the elder
Latimer leaned forward and said that he did not know that there were any
speed limits on the main roads of France. He sounded a little indignant.

The policeman said that he knew now; took out his notebook, thinking as he did so that the gentlemen in the back looked a bit odd, somehow.
Dark-skinned. Creoles or something of the kind. Then something in James'
accent recurred to him and he asked what nationality they were.

"English," said Hawkes rapidly in French. "The driver is English too.
It's my fault, I ought to have noticed the sign, but I didn't."

"Ah," said the policeman. "English, that explains all." He put away
his notebook and leaned forward to look into the car. "Listen, messieurs.
When you see by the roadside a round red sign with a number on it—a
number on it—"

His voice trailed off and he drew back. Then the familiar phrase of
the French police rose in his mind to rescue him from embarrassment.
"May I see your papers, please?"

The occupants of the car, including Wilkins, dived hands into pockets for their passports and James' came out first. The cuff of a coat sleeve
appeared at the window and, four inches in front of it, a British passport
unsupported, resting upon the air. The policeman set his jaw.

"Some joke, I assume," he said loftily. "Circus turn, are you? All
done with wires."

He took hold of the passport, and his hand encountered fingers which
he could feel but not see. He stepped back, dropped the passport in the
road, turned round, and walked heavily away. Wilkins leapt out, retrieved
the passport, and returned to his seat.

"Drive on, Wilkins," said Hawkes. "I don't think he wants to talk to
us after all."

"Very good, sir," said Wilkins, and moved off. "If I may be permitted
the comment, sir, there are moments when an element of the supernatural
may have practical applications."

Hawkes looked back through the rear window as they drove away. A
solid blue-clad form plodded steadily up the village street and did not
once look behind it.

A little later Wilkins nodded ahead to where fretted pinnacles rose
into the air above the roofs of houses.

"Chartres, sir. Only a couple of miles, now."

"I was conscious of it," said James gleefully. "I was aware of returning strength and energy. How say you, Charles?"

"Yes, sir," said Charles emphatically, "that certainly is so. Mr. Hawkes, tell us, are we becoming more fit for public view?"

Hawkes turned round; there were the two familiar faces, one olive-skinned and the other sanguine, fully visible again.

"Oh yes," he said, "a great improvement. You don't look perfectly solid yet, but I can see you quite plainly. Much, much better."

"Another couple of miles and the cure will, I judge, be complete," said James. "This has been a lesson to me; we will not run such a risk again, how say you, Charles?"

"I am of your opinion, James. Away with so much delicacy, away with tact. Cousin Richard can hold his lady's hand after we are gone back. My stars, yes!"

When the car drew up before the hotel called after Le Grand Monarque, the Latimers stepped briskly out. They were as vivid and vital as ever; their movements were energetic and their carriage debonair. They wore their hats with an air, slightly tilted. James' face had its normal high color and his fair hair was faintly tinged with auburn; Charles' browner skin had the glow of perfect health and his dark eyes were full of laughter. Richard Scroby was standing in the doorway; beside him, with her arm through his, was the girl Virginia Townsend.

Miss Scroby was having a very happy time in Paris, contrary to expectations. She had arrived knowing no one, expecting no pleasure from the visit, and with an unpleasant duty before her, and Fate had thrown across her path the young man Philippe Morand. He was helpful, courteous, and unobtrusive, but he had a wonderful knack of appearing exactly when he was wanted. Also, he seemed to have no other engagements and no particular business although he talked vaguely about his affairs.

Angela Scroby was no fool and she knew perfectly well that a young man like Pépi would not for nothing dance attendance upon a woman easily old enough to be his mother. She turned those penetrating gray eyes steadily upon him, but Pépi, inwardly quaking, managed to smile back. She was his "prospect" and he was not going to be put off.

"Listen, Monsieur Morand," she said at the end of two days' acquaintance.

"I am all ears, madame."

"You will forgive me if I am frank. You do not seem to me to be engaged in any steady employment, you know Paris extremely well, and

I do not believe that you are in particularly affluent circumstances."

"I am not rich, madame, that is true, but you have not heard me complain, have you? It is also true that I have no regular employment at the moment; I am waiting for news of a fresh opening."

"I do not wish to pry into your affairs," said Miss Scroby primly. "I was about to suggest something. I am here in Paris knowing nothing of the place or the language. Will you be my courier? On a reasonable salary, of course. You will take me about and show me Paris; we might make excursions to Versailles or Fontainebleau. I understand that those places deserve a visit. I shall, of course, pay all expenses besides your salary."

Pépi accepted in a few modest and well-turned phrases, having the intelligence not to appear too eager. He was not sure how long he would be in Paris, but while he was he would be willingly and delightedly at Madame's service. In the background of his mind he was wondering whether his guardian angel had at last decided to get down to a spot of work or whether there was some horrid catch in this business which would appear later.

So they went about together and both enjoyed it.

Miss Scroby told herself every day that tomorrow she would go to the Lune d'Italie and have it out with Richard. When tomorrow came she and Pépi hired a car and went to Barbizon, Malmaison, or the Forest of Chantilly or amused themselves at exhibitions of modern art.

Pépi told himself that this time was not only pleasant and mildly profitable but was not being wasted. He was, he said to himself, preparing the ground. Presently he would arrange some good scheme which would bring in a really substantial reward. Something foolproof, something brilliant, for Miss Scroby evidently had plenty of money. Let it go for the moment. He found, to his surprise, that he liked Miss Scroby, her blunt comments amused him, and—he told himself that he must be sickening for something insidious—her transparent and instinctive honesty had a charm all its own. He sat in a bar one night after she had retired and thought this over. Miss Scroby was truthful and honest because she had never had any need to be anything else; how nice to be like that. She was secure, that was why. An accepted place and enough money. Anyone could be honest if they had security and enough money.

Of course, some people simply could not be honest however well they were placed. Men of wealth and rank could be twisters, but such men were twisted to start with. Cranks. Misfits. Pépi told himself that there was nothing twisted about him and that he would find it pleasant to be truthful and secure and honest and sufficiently wealthy. They all went together and were all equally improbable.

He had had dreams like this before.

Perhaps Miss Scroby could be induced to part with enough money to enable him to make a fresh start. If she could be induced to buy something; a house or a business—a hotel business, he could talk about hotels—and entrust him with the purchase money, or some of it. A thumping big deposit, for instance, in something negotiable that he could turn into cash. Twenty minutes later he would be out of Paris and never come back.

He sighed inaudibly, pulled a newspaper towards him, and began to study the column headed: "Businesses for Sale."

Miss Scroby, for her part, was enjoying every minute of her days. She could not, in fact, remember ever having been so carelessly happy before since the early days of carefree childhood. She had expected to find Paris shallow, meretricious, reprehensible; instead she found it gay and charming. The weather was warm and sunny; flags fluttered, bands played, and fountains tossed diamond plumes in the air. If she saw posters advertising entertainments in what she would have described as "dubious taste" she averted her eyes and considered that foreign standards are not the same as ours at home and in any case it was no business of hers. She was not responsible; for the first time for many years she was not responsible for anything, not for a small boy left in her care, not for the management of a household, not even for the welfare of a village. She was free, and the sensation was extraordinarily pleasant.

So pleasant, indeed, that she began to sympathize with Richard. It dawned upon her quite suddenly one morning in the Place de la Concorde that Richard too would naturally delight in freedom and that she had consistently denied it to him. From the best of motives, no doubt, but a good motive is not all. Far from it. She stopped suddenly, frowning, and Pépi deferentially touched her arm.

"What is it, madame? Are you not well?"

"I am an ill-tempered overbearing old hag!" she said fiercely.

"Oh, madame!"

"Let us go and sit upon some terrace and drink a cup of coffee," she said.

"This way," said Pépi unhesitatingly, and piloted her across the road to a café, where they sat in a sunlit corner and watched the traffic swirling past. The coffee was brought; Pépi lit her cigarette and his own and waited.

"I have a nephew," she began, and, once started, it all came out. She had brought him up, she felt responsible for him, he was financially inde-

pendent; when he left the University he took a flat—and a manservant—
and collected snuffboxes and went in for boxing. He started that at school,
and so on. Then there was the horrid affair at his flat when that man tried
to break in, a French criminal called Toni le Chat. Scroby had hit him on
the head; he had fallen out of the window and been arrested by the police.
The publicity, the lurking gang probably bent on revenge, the disgraceful
stocking, the flight to Paris. She had discovered where he was staying and
that he had repeatedly been seen in company with a girl. No nice girl
would wear stockings like that and why was it on the floor in Scroby's
flat?

Pépi listened to all this with an undeviating attention which Miss
Scroby found most satisfying, as well she might, for it was perfectly
genuine.

"You are afraid, madame, that the friends of this criminal may wish
revenge upon Monsieur Scroby? Why should they?"

"It was through my nephew that the wretched man was caught, you
see."

"But is he a detective—is he of the police?"

"Dear me, no. Why should he be? He came home from a dinner, not
feeling at all well, the fish had upset him—"

"Deplorable," murmured Pépi, controlling the corners of his mouth
with difficulty.

"And he saw this man climbing in at the window. So Richard picked
up a tall vase I had given him and hit the man on the head and he fell
down. Richard simply went straight to bed. Then the police came and the
newspapermen—dreadful, all that publicity. I saw it in the paper and I
was greatly incensed. Unreasonably so, Monsieur Morand, I see it now. I
have been harsh with Richard and he has come to Paris to get away from
me. If he is with undesirable companions it is my fault."

There was a long pause. Miss Scroby looked away with eyes which
saw nothing of what they rested upon, and Pépi was furiously thinking.
They had been hopelessly wrong, he and Fingers and Jules, in supposing
Scroby to be of the police. He, Pépi, had been wrong, for it was his idea
and the others had believed it. That was why they were planning to knock
Scroby on the head and drop him in the Seine. They might have done it
already; they might do it tonight. Murder, and for no reason, and all his
fault, and how this Englishwoman would grieve. Murder, and it would lie
at his door.

Pépi moved sharply and Miss Scroby looked round.

"I came to Paris to have it out with him," she said, "and every day I have said that tomorrow will do. I have been funking it, as schoolboys say. Now I am not angry with him any more but I am still funking it. I ought to go to the Lune d'Italie and tell him I am sorry, but what will he say? You are a young man not so much older than Richard—how old are you?"

"Thirty-four."

"Eleven years older."

"Much more than that," said Pépi impulsively, and she looked at him and nodded.

"If you were in his place, would you laugh at me?"

"No," said Pépi explosively, and said to himself: "What's the matter with me? That's twice I've told the truth."

"I don't know what to do," said Angela Scroby, and caught herself up. "That is not true. I do know what I ought to do but I cannot bring myself to do it. If that girl is a bad type—what shall I do?"

"Listen, madame," said Pépi "since you deign to ask my counsel. This stocking, I think you have the wrong ideas. Madame, I was trained as an hotelier, I was headwaiter, in another year or two I should have been undermanager—never mind that. In my charge were the table appointments, the silver to be cleaned every day, early in the morning. What with? Madame, I made an arrangement with a rag merchant for silk stockings—nylon stockings—soft and fine as a spider's web. I can see our pantry now, the long table spread thick with newspapers over felt; the two other waiters, the four apprentice waiters and myself in charge, all polishing away like mad with these so lovely wisps of gossamer. It seemed wicked to use them so, but what can one do with an odd stocking? I will tell you, madame. One cleans the silver with it. *V'là tout.*"

She looked at him again, the familiar forthright look which, Pépi always felt, penetrated his forehead to the brain behind it and read all his thoughts. Nonsense, of course, but that was the impression he always received. On this occasion, for the very first time, he did not mind it.

"It could be true," she said. "Wilkins kept the silver very well."

Pépi made a mental note that Wilkins was the name of the manservant.

"As for the young lady, madame, would you care—I do not wish to intrude—"

"What?"

"Would it serve you at all if I were to make a few careful enquiries about her—if, indeed, Monsieur Scroby has a friend in a young lady?"

"But could you do that without its becoming known that someone was enquiring? I could not bear it if he found out that I was spying on him—"

She broke off and blushed awkwardly, for she had done it once and was now upon the point of doing it again, but Pépi, much as he admired her ethical standards, thought this was too much. Beautiful, but silly.

"But, madame! To enquire into the antecedents of one who may become a member of the family, that is a duty!"

She looked at him again, in surprise this time, for it was years since anyone had addressed Angela Scroby on the subject of her duty.

"You may be right," she said, and smiled suddenly.

"Thank heavens, madame! I thought you were not going to smile at all today. No, it is not spying. It is to find out the young lady's name, her family if possible and a little about her circumstances, that is all. You would like me to do this?"

She would. She would like it done at once, for now that it had been suggested she could not wait for the answer.

"But you will be careful? I cannot imagine how you will go about it."

"Leave it to me, madame. I have methods of finding out about people; I have contacts in many places."

He put her in a taxi to return to the Couronne de Navarre and himself walked away, wiping his brow and feeling a little weak at the knees.

"This truth-speaking, is it an infectious disease? I tell her I am hotelier, I tell her I can find out about people; one of these days I sit and hear myself telling her I am a con man and I am after her money. Then they put me in a home. This Scroby, is he still alive?"

CHAPTER XV
Hot News

SCROBY'S car, which had conveyed the Latimers, Hawkes, and Wilkins to Chartres, arrived there between four and five in the evening. After the greetings and cries of astonishment were finished, Hawkes said that he ought to be getting back. There were, no doubt, trains; if the hotel proprietor had a railway timetable in his office—

Scroby said it was nonsense. Absolute bilge, Hawkes talking about rushing back to Paris when he had only just arrived. "Are you," asked Scroby lyrically, "a tennis ball that you have to bounce back as fast as you came? Don't be silly. I want you to get to know Virginia; you've got to meet her mother. I tell you, Hawkes, this is a great day. Cousin James and Cousin Charles, I have news for you. As representatives of my family, greet my future wife. She has agreed to marry me; she can't be right in her head, but we'll overlook that, shall we? Virginia darling."

James bent over Virginia's hand and produced without a second's hesitation a beautiful little speech in which all generations of the Scroby-Latimer connection, past, present, and to come, assembled together like the final curtain of a musical comedy to salute and embrace within their visionary ranks the fairest flower among them all. He then kissed her formally upon the forehead and retired to make room for Charles, who kissed her hand instead.

"Miss Virginia, ma'am, how happy you have made us all. Richard here is certainly a lucky fellow, yes, ma'am."

After which Hawkes' hearty pump-handling and "Many happy years, both of you," seemed a page out of another book.

"You're staying here tonight, aren't you, Hawkes? You simply must, we've got a celebration dinner laid on."

Hawkes said he would be delighted and looked it, but his manner was a trifle absent and a few minutes later he had slipped unnoticed from the room to hurry along to the manager's office.

"Is there anyone in Chartres who can take photographs?"

"But scores, monsieur. Chartres lives largely upon the sale of photographs. Our Cathedral—"

"I didn't mean gargoyles. I mean, is there anyone who does 'candid camera' shots—flashlight photos of people at parties, you know?"

"There is a man who takes pictures for the local Press."

"That will do. Name and address?"

The manager supplied both.

"Excellent, thanks. Oh, one more thing. Have you a typewriter which you could be so obliging as to lend me for an hour or so this evening? I have some urgent work tonight."

"With pleasure, monsieur. This one," said the manager, indicating a machine upon a side table.

"A thousand thanks, I will come for it later," said Hawkes, turning to go. "Oh, by the way, I can have a room here tonight, can I?"

"A moment," said the manager, opening his register while Hawkes hovered impatiently in the doorway. "Yes, a small room on the second floor with—"

"That will do, I'll take it," said Hawkes, and was gone. Charles Latimer in the lounge, exchanging polite conversation with Virginia's mother, saw the journalist pass through the hall with rapid steps and out into the street. Charles caught James Latimer's eye and began to disengage himself from Mrs. Townsend.

"This seems to be a charming old town, ma'am, from the little we saw of it driving in."

"Oh, it is indeed. Have you not been here before, Major Latimer?"

"Never, ma'am, but my cousin is more widely traveled than I. Do you know this town of old, James?"

"I passed through it many years since and paid a visit, which I shall always remember, to the Cathedral. Would you care, Charles, to accept me as your cicerone for a brief tour? There is time, I think, before dinner—Mrs. Townsend, can we prevail upon you to accompany us?"

But she excused herself; they had spent the afternoon sightseeing. "It's all just too marvelous," she said, "but didn't those wonderful old Gothic builders just adore steps? I guess they probably symbolize something like the upward struggle of the soul to higher things and don't think I can't appreciate all that beauty because I certainly do, Mr. Latimer, but there are moments when a woman realizes what a blessing it is to have been born into an age of elevators. I think I'll enjoy my evening more if I just go and put my feet up for half an hour before I change for dinner."

She smiled and nodded and moved away; James and Charles strolled out together into the street.

"What is it, Charles?"

"The enterprising Mr. Hawkes. He seems plaguey busy about something and I wondered what it might be."

"But could it possibly be any concern of ours?"

"It could, James, indeed it could. Yes, sir. Mr. Hawkes is a journalist."

"What of that?"

"Mr. Hawkes writes for one of the English newspapers—among other matters, no doubt—a weekly article called, I understand, 'In France Today,' or some such. Richard told me Hawkes goes about to observe whatever may be strange enough to be of interest to his English readers; he has but just returned from a tour of France for the purpose of gathering information."

"That could be interesting if well observed," said James judicially. "Informative. Educational."

"Certainly. Yes, sir. Mr. Hawkes is, I judge, always on the *qui-vive* for a good story." They paused upon the edge of the pavement and tilted their hats back to gaze up at the Cathedral soaring above them into the evening sky. "James, does it not occur to you that we, by our antics this afternoon, provided him with the story of a lifetime?"

James abandoned the contemplation of sublimity and frowned.

"Charles, surely not. Consider what you suggest. No gentleman of any delicacy of feeling would make public in the national Press the physical peculiarities of a fellow guest! He was with us in Richard's car, and self-invited at that—"

"That was what first put me on my guard, James. What? This young man is back in Paris after an absence of some time, and he abandons all his affairs to take a country drive with total strangers, why? Look, James, step back within this doorway. He is hurrying into that stationer's shop; if he comes out with a packet of writing paper—"

They waited a few minutes and were rewarded by seeing Hawkes come out with a square flat parcel under his arm. He turned towards the Place des Epars and their hotel, walking fast.

"I have an idea, James," laughed Charles. "I, too, will buy writing paper and a pen—hotel pens were ever vile."

"Even now," protested James, following Charles into the shop, "we do not know the subject of his essay."

"If it be inoffensive, there is no harm done. He may publish essays about the antiquities of Chartres in every paper from China to Peru. Will you take a wager on it, Cousin?"

They returned to the Grand Monarque just in time to see Hawkes staggering up to his room with a typewriter not of the sort called portable. The Latimers merely exchanged glances and went to their own room to make ready for dinner.

They had the sort of dinner which a really good country hotel in France can put on when it tries. The hotel staff were thrilled to the marrow with the romance which had declared itself under their roof; a celebration dinner was desired, was it? But certainly. The cook should put himself upon his mettle and the manager would stake his reputation as hotelier upon the result. He went into conference with James Latimer about wines, since Scroby was far too ecstatic to talk sense. When the six guests entered the dining-room they were received like royalty and bowed to their flower-decked table upon which Virginia's place was encircled with rosebuds. The soup came and went and the company were attacking the famous *patés de Chartres* when a young man in a creased blue suit came rapidly across the room, stopped a little short of their table, and smiled engagingly upon them.

He carried a rather large camera with the reflector of a flashbulb at-
tachment sticking up at the top. Mrs. Townsend and her daughter, who
were completely accustomed to having flashlight photographs taken at
parties, assumed graceful poses and waited for it, Scroby grinned cheerfully, and Hawkes watched the party from one side. The Latimers were
not interested in photography and had never encountered a flashbulb before; they glanced up with merely courteous interest and wondered vaguely
what the young man was about.

The next moment a blinding flash went off right in their faces. The
young man was in the act of fitting a second flashbulb when Mrs. Townsend
stopped him.

"Thank you," she said, waving the photographer away with a burst of
silvery laughter, "thank you, young man, that will do. I know this kind of
thing goes on all the time and anyone who is a genuine celebrity has them
shot off at them simply all day and all night till I assume they get so used
to it they just don't notice it at all, or do they? I always say, don't I,
Virginia, that if I were a celebrity I'd just have to rush away and lock
myself in the bathroom because the way those things give me spots before the eyes is just nobody's business. Mr. Latimer, you look quite pale."

"I was startled, ma'am," admitted James. He picked up his glass and
swallowed the contents; the photographer bowed to the company and
hurried away and the dinner resumed its delectable course.

Hawkes slipped away as soon after the dinner as was decently possible, murmuring an excuse about having "something to see to." Charles
was not long after him; when James Latimer came up to their room later
he found his cousin at the writing table, covering sheet after sheet with
his even, slanting, pointed writing.

"Well?" said James, and Charles looked round with a laugh.

"It is very well, Cousin. Mr. Hawkes is in the throes of composition
and is, I opine, enjoying himself. He started with the séance and our message and leapt from there to our complete normality in Scroby's room
yesterday, a normality only marred by the inexplicable arrival of Ulysses.
He writes quite capably in the modern manner; I will maintain that Mr.
Hawkes can tell a story, yes, sir. Go you, James, and look over his shoulder; I warrant you will be entertained. I have paid him three separate
visits."

"Knowing, as he does, what we are, does he not betray any consciousness of your immaterial presence?"

"Not a jot, Cousin," said Charles cheerfully, "unless you breathe upon the back of his neck; that makes him shiver."

James laughed and went from the room without needing to open the door; though there were guests about in the corridors none saw him go or return, nor did Hawkes' flying fingers upon the typewriter keys falter or make any mistake. James Latimer materialized again beside Charles' chair and said that in his opinion the thing was an outrage. "No reticences, sir, but a barefaced attempt to make money out of private affairs into which he intruded himself unasked."

"Calm yourself, James, the attempt will not succeed."

"Had it not been for your quick wits, Charles, it would have done so and I none the wiser. What are you writing?"

Charles' eyebrows rose and his long mouth curled up at the corners.

"Why, Cousin," he drawled, "the sight of so much literary energy fired me with emulation. Yes, sir. I reckon that I have seen many things in my time which would make a good story; in short, I was seized with the journalistic itch myself. This, sir, is an eyewitness account of the Battle of Richmond."

James considered this.

"I do not doubt, Charles, that your account of that battle would have high evidential and historic value, but in view of its having taken place over ninety years ago it can scarcely be called 'news.' "

"You are, as always, entirely in the right, Cousin."

"Then why—"

"I thought to myself that a number of written sheets would come in usefully for a certain purpose if occasion should arise. It may not, in which case—since I cannot endure my maiden effort to be entirely wasted—I will sign it with my full name, regiment, and rank and post it to the Congress of the United States of America. Just a moment, James, while I pen the last lines and then let us see how my rival is progressing."

Charles bent once more over his manuscript while his cousin drew back the curtains to look out of the window. Presently the faint scratching of the pen ceased and James looked round to see Charles, with a brow furrowed with concentration, reading his article and reviewing the punctuation.

"These damned commas," he murmured.

He straightened the sheets of paper, folded them neatly, and stood up.

"Well?" he said. "Shall we go?"

Hawkes had arrived at much the same point. When the Latimers, unheralded and unseen, arrived in his room he was reading rapidly but carefully through the sheets of typescript and making small neat corrections here and there. Charles noticed, with a glee of which the writer was naturally unaware, that even a practiced journalist sometimes reorganizes his punctuation. When Hawkes had finished he addressed a large envelope to the *London Record,* folded the sheets, slipped them in, and stretched himself as though he were tired of sitting. Quite suddenly, for no apparent reason, he spun round in his chair and looked sharply behind him. There was, of course, no one to be seen.

On a small table near the door there was a tray with a half bottle of Dubonnet upon it, a bottle of soda water, a bowl of ice largely melted, and a tumbler. Hawkes strolled across and prepared himself a drink; the soda water needed to be opened and the floating ice fished out with a spoon. When it was to his liking he turned, glass in hand, and drank the contents at a draught. Then he looked at his watch and began to mix himself another. Dubonnet, ice, and soda water are a harmless mixture, but one would have said that he was uneasy about something, for twice during the simple operation he turned to look searchingly about the room.

There came a knock at the door and Hawkes opened it to admit the young man who had taken the flashlight photograph.

"Oh, good," said Hawkes. "I have only this moment finished. I left the envelope open for the print."

"I am desolated, monsieur," said the photographer, "but there is something wrong with it." He took a print from an envelope and showed it to Hawkes. "You see, it is quite clear and sharp of the two ladies, the Englishman, and yourself, but the two gentlemen you particularly wanted, they are not there. Look. There are, as it were, two gaps."

"Strange," said Hawkes, and took the print under the light to look at it closely.

"You see," said the photographer, following him, "there is as it were a slight blur in one place, as though the gentlemen had dodged quickly, but that is not possible, it was too quick, I had my eyes upon them when I pressed the button."

"No," said Hawkes. "I mean, yes."

"And in the other case, the dark gentleman held a glass in his fingers, did he not? Yes, and there is the glass. There is something a little odd about that too, for if you look closely it appears as though the glass were a couple of inches above the table."

"It does," said Hawkes in a heavy voice, "doesn't it?"

"I regret infinitely, monsieur. I wish now that I had taken a second, but the elder lady did not wish it."

"How much do I owe you?"

"But nothing, monsieur. The photograph is, in the main respect, a failure."

"That is not your fault," said Hawkes, and paid him.

"A thousand thanks, Monsieur is generous. I cannot understand at all what happened."

"I cannot explain it—and if I did, you would not believe me," said Hawkes, picking up his letter and sticking down the flap.

"Pardon, monsieur?"

"It is nothing. I have some stamps, here they are."

"Can I perhaps save Monsieur a journey by posting his letter?"

"I will come down with you," said Hawkes. "I think a turn in the fresh air will do me good."

The Latimers returned to their own room and Charles handed a number of typewritten sheets to his cousin.

"Do you care to peruse these, James?"

"This nonsense? No, I thank you. Do you wish to keep them? No, then let us dispose of the impertinence." James tore the sheets into small pieces and dropped them in the wastepaper basket.

" 'So perish all traitors?' " laughed Charles. "Cousin, do you think that the editor of the *London Record,* that great paper, will publish an eyewitness account of the Battle of Richmond?"

When the Latimers came down to breakfast the following morning Scroby told them that Hawkes had left by an early train. He had remembered an important engagement in Paris.

Pépi returned to Miss Scroby with information about her nephew. The young lady was a Miss Virginia Townsend who was staying with her mother, Mrs. Townsend, at the Hôtel Scribe. The ladies were all that could be desired of the most respectable; they had come to Paris because the Miss was studying antiques and they spent most of their days visiting museums and collections.

Miss Scroby's look of incredulous delight, dawning slowly over a face grimly set to receive bad news, was at once comic and touching. Pépi saw it.

"You are very fond of him, madame."

"Naturally," she said sharply. "These ladies, are they English?"

"American, madame. They come from—I am not sure whether I have this right, it sounds to me like a confusion. The young lady's name is Virginia; is there a place called Virginia also—"

"There is. Not a place, but a state. They come from Virginia, do they?

Townsends of Virginia, I remember, yes. From near Charlottesville. When I was a young girl and went to balls in Richmond—that is the capital of the state of Virginia, Monsieur Morand—there were Townsends also who used to attend, Army men, in uniform. Dear me, yes. Tall young men with a pretty sister a little older than I was. I remember, yes. So she is one of them."

Angela Scroby retired into the past and Pépi waited until she chose to return.

"What is she like, have you seen her?"

"No, madame. They are all away from Paris at the moment; they are at Chartres for a few days. Not for long, since the rooms are being kept on at the Scribe and also at the Lune d'Italie—"

"My nephew has gone to Chartres also?"

"But, yes, madame. He and two cousins of his named Latimer who are also staying at the Lune d'Italie."

Miss Scroby nodded. "I know about them, I remember them as boys. They are Virginians too."

"One is American, madame, yes. The other, they say, is English."

"Oh? Oh, really. In that case, I do not know him. They are a large family."

"Indeed, madame."

"Since my nephew is away, I need not for a few days torment my conscience about going to see him. Monsieur Morand, I have been thinking."

"Yes, madame?"

"I like Paris."

"I am enchanted to hear it, madame."

"Not only do I like it, but it is good for me. I have lived so long in the same place that I have got into a rut."

"A—pardon me?"

"A rut. A deep narrow track made by the wheel of a heavy vehicle in soft mud. A figure of speech to denote one who, like me, lives in the same place, seeing the same people and doing the same things. A narrow life with narrow interests and a narrow mind."

"Oh, madame," said Pépi with a deprecating smile.

"I have decided to spend at least some part of every year in Paris. I propose to take a small flat. Can you recommend to me a reputable house agent?"

He could and did. The next few days were spent in inspecting flats of all shapes, sizes, and states of repair. Some of these places they visited together; some Miss Scroby, who was getting to know Paris, visited alone.

"It is of no use," she said at last. "They are all ridiculously and dishonestly expensive. None of the places I have seen are worth a fraction of the grossly inflated prices that are asked for them."

"No, madame, but rents are high in Paris. Besides that, I know that it is nearly impossible for the English to get their money out of England to stay abroad for long times."

"That does not trouble me, fortunately. I am American by birth and my money comes from there. One can always get dollars."

Pépi drew a long breath. Here it was, at last, the prospect for which he had worked so patiently. He had spread the net so tactfully and at last the fish had swum in. American dollars, of course. He opened his mouth and shut it again, and Miss Scroby watched him with those piercing gray eyes.

He seemed to have lost his voice—*allons, Pépi!*

He cleared his throat and even then his voice sounded to him like a croak.

"Has it ever occurred to you, chere madame, to buy a hotel?"

"No. Why should I?"

"Madame could then have a small suite reserved for her own use. Bedroom, sitting room, bathroom, for whenever you wish to visit Paris."

"But I can take a small suite—or a single room—at any hotel in Paris at any time without having to buy the hotel to—"

"*Bien sûr,* madame, but you will have to pay for it, excuse me. If you buy the hotel your suite would come out of the profits."

"I see," said Miss Scroby thoughtfully. "Yes."

"And it would be, always, a place of your own."

A day or two later Hawkes, at his flat in Paris, received a large envelope from the *London Record.* It contained a number of sheets covered with handwriting and a note from the subeditor. "Dear Hawkes, I return these in case they are of some value to you. We don't want them. Your weekly article not received," and a postscript: "Put more water with it in future."

Hawkes, with bolting eyes, settled down to read a dramatic eyewitness account of the Battle of Richmond. When he had finished he laid down the sheets and stared moodily out of the window.

"And there goes my best story," he said bitterly.

CHAPTER XVI
Hôtel Akela

"BUT WHY?" asked Virginia. "I don't understand. Did she beat you when you were a little boy?"

"Oh no, I don't think so," said Scroby vaguely. "I had a nanny at one time who used to spank me, but Aunt Angela sent her away. No, it's because she always knows best and, if you stop to think, she's usually right. Except, of course, about Millicent Biggleswade. Apart from that, she's a very sensible woman, my aunt. If you disagree with her, she makes your ideas look so horribly silly. They are, too, by the time she's done with them. But it's so much nicer to be silly off your own bat than to be sensible all the time at someone else's bidding. One gets so tired of being sensible."

Virginia nodded.

"And now she's come to Paris," added Scroby, "just when I was so happy."

"Darling, haven't you ever defied her?"

"Not really, not till I came away to Paris. I know," said Scroby, coloring up, "this must sound awfully soppy and spineless to you, but I do find it quite impossible to be rude to Aunt Angela; I mean, one simply can't say 'Shut up' or 'Mind your own business,' and nothing less does any good. The trouble is, of course, that I'm really fond of her; sounds silly, I know, but all those years when I was a kid— I do wish she'd realize that I'm grown up. I won't be bossed about any more," he said with alarming energy, "especially now I've got you. She's a worry and I don't want to be worried."

Virginia sat and looked at him for a long minute and then got up with an air of decision.

"I'm going upstairs to pack."

"Pack? What—what—where—Virginia, you don't mean—"

"I shall pack and so will you, or Wilkins will do it for you. Mother also will pack and so, if they like, can your cousins. We are going back to Paris, my pet; when we get there we will find out where your aunt is staying and we will go and call on her. You will present me. 'Aunt Angela, meet Virginia, my fiancée.' Then I shall advance with hands outstretched, like this, and say, 'Miss Scroby—may I call you Aunt Angela? I want to thank you for—for Richard.' Then I shall sob on her shoulder and you'd better go out for half an hour."

"But if—"

"No 'but if.' Have you ever sobbed on her shoulder?"

Scroby thought. "Not since I was six and the farmer's dog killed my kitten."

"No, I suppose you couldn't keep it up. You leave it to me."

The hotel which Pépi had in mind was a small one in the Rue Vignon, a good central position near the Madeleine with a Métro station nearby. The Rue Vignon is just off the Boulevard de la Madeleine and is within easy reach of the Rue de la Paix, the Place Vendôme, the Rue de Rivoli, and other delights, but it is itself a narrow, rather dark street of small shops and cafés. The Hôtel Akela had some twenty bedrooms, a dining-saloon, and a lounge so small that it was in fact merely a bar with ambitions, and there was no lift.

"The proprietor," said Pépi, "is an elderly man who suffers in his legs, he wishes to retire to the country and not stand about on his poor legs any more at all for the rest of his life. Also, his wife has died of late. He wishes to go to the country to live with his married daughter."

Pépi and Miss Scroby were standing within a shop doorway opposite to the hotel.

"It looks as though it has not been painted since he was an active young man," said Miss Scroby looking up at the windows, "and those shutters look quite dangerous."

"It requires redecoration, yes, madame, but the structure is sound, I believe. A man I know was the desk clerk there at one time; he says the stairs and walls are of an unbelievable solidity."

"And the price, about—?"

"Nine million five hundred thousand francs, madame."

"Nine thousand five hundred pounds sterling, nearly. What's the matter with it?"

"It is a rumor, madame. The story goes that these three houses opposite are to be taken down to build a subpower station for the electric light. Madame knows? There is one in the Rue Caumartin, we passed it the other day when I pointed out the Hôtel de la Lune d'Italie. Madame asked me where the roaring noise came from."

"I remember. One could not have a hotel opposite to a noise like that. Not unless one wished to occupy an entire hotel all alone."

"A little melancholy, that! No, indeed, madame, but the story is not true. The idea has been destroyed, on better thoughts. I know that, a friend of mine works in the offices of the Electricity Company of Paris. There will be no subpower station here, and so the little flower shop, the hair-dressing shop, and the delicatessen shop here may go on living."

"I see, yes. I think I will go across and look at it. I will say that I am looking for rooms for friends."

"Yes, madame. If I might suggest—"

"What?"

"It would be better not to say that Madame is American. That word, it is like yeast, it makes prices rise."

She smiled at him, asked him to wait for her, and crossed the road to the Hôtel Akela. She had remembered or acquired enough French by that time to make simple enquiries.

Pépi strolled away and drank a glass of wine at a café within view. He was out in the street again and waiting for her before she returned.

"Well, madame?"

"A nice little hotel and very well found."

"Very—well—pardon?"

"Found. Provided. Furnished. Fitted up."

"I learn more English every day," smiled Pépi.

"I hate his wallpapers and his paint is horrid, but there is a little self-contained suite on the first floor. He called it 'for the bride.' " Miss Scroby chuckled grimly. "A bridal suite, we should say in England. At present it has green striped wallpaper and liver-colored paint, but that could easily be altered."

Pépi drew a sudden long breath and let it out carefully. "Then you like it, madame?"

"There are probably some horrid drawbacks which will appear upon further investigation, but I think it is worth looking into, yes." She turned those piercing grey eyes upon him and again he had to brace himself to meet them.

"Would it serve you, madame, if I were to make the first enquiries? I should not, by myself, give the impression of having much money to spend."

"I should be most grateful if you would. He has a few words of English, the old man; I managed to see some of the rooms, but there were many questions I should not know how to ask. You could ask to see the kitchens and so on, you are able to judge them better than I."

"When would you like me to go, madame?"

"Now? Can you spare the time? I will go back to my hotel now; perhaps you will come there and tell me all about it."

He put her into a taxi and returned alone to the Hôtel Akela. It was all going according to plan, if only he did not spoil it now.

A little over an hour later he came out of the hotel and walked slowly up the street, thinking so deeply as to be quite unaware of his surroundings. He had made all the necessary enquiries; what shook him to the core of his being was that matters could not possibly have been more favorable for his schemes if he had arranged them himself. He would not have to tell Miss Scroby even one little lie, not even the smallest modification of the truth. He was so accustomed to twisting facts to suit his own ends that the naked truth seemed to him almost indecent, as though he had suddenly found himself half dressed in the Rue de la Paix.

He walked on. Truly, his guardian angel had been working overtime to put this chance in his way. Since it is not far from the Rue Vignon to the Chaussée d'Antin, he was turning in between the shops to the hotel entrance before he had cleared his mind.

After putting his foot three times upon the lowest step of the stairway up to the Couronne de Navarre's front door and taking it off again, Pépi lost his temper with himself and dashed up two at a time. Miss Scroby was sitting in a corner of the lounge waiting for him; the place was empty at that hour.

"How good of you," she said with her unexpectedly pleasant smile, "to take all this trouble for me."

"A pleasure, madame—"

"Please sit down."

"Thank you. I saw the old man, the proprietor, and he showed me all over the hotel. I told him that I was considering buying the place; if Madame will forgive me, I thought I could get a better price that way. I saw all the service rooms and kitchen quarters as well as the rest of the house. Some of the kitchen things need replacement; I think the gas stove must be one of the first ever made, madame, but the china and glass and silver for the dining room are very good." He went on to give a thorough report of the place from top to bottom; a leaking gutter in one place had made one wall damp; the top-floor bathroom was very shabby, and so on. "I think that those are all the faults, madame."

"Thank you, yes. Please go on."

"The old monsieur wants to get out at once; that is, he needs the money at once and will go out as soon as he receives it. His daughter wishes to buy a small business in Bergerac, where she lives, and the chance will not long remain open. I beat him down a hundred thousand francs for a quick sale, madame, if the deal is closed within twenty-four hours—it is, of course, as madame pleases."

"The hotel staff—" she began.

"Will stay on if desired. I saw most of them and liked what I saw; certainly they keep the place well."

"I see. Well, that makes the price—"

"Nine million four hundred thousand francs."

"And he wants the money at once. How soon is 'at once' in Paris?"

"A deposit of ten per cent, madame, nine hundred and forty thousand francs within twenty-four hours."

"And the balance?"

"Within a week."

"I see." Miss Scroby rose from her chair and walked up and down the room while Pépi stood and waited, not even looking at her.

"I suppose," she said eventually, "if I were to change my mind—if I did not wish to keep the place—I could sell it again without much loss. If it proved to be a worry to me in any way."

"I believe, myself," said Pépi, "that Madame would make a profit on the deal, especially after the place has been done up. The old monsieur is in a hurry for the money, he cannot wait."

"And there is absolutely no chance of the power station being built opposite? You are quite sure?"

"Quite sure, madame. Absolutely none."

Another turn up and down the room and then a rather excited laugh.

"It may not be very sensible of me," she said, "but one can get tired of being always sensible. I suppose he will take a check?"

"He wants the deposit in cash, madame. The balance, of course, by check or banker's order."

"The deposit in cash? Why?"

Pépi laughed.

"In France, madame, it is thought wiser not to allow one's bank to know how much money one has. The taxes, you know. He will pay for the business in Bergerac by check, no doubt, but this cash he will keep, yes?"

"Do you have many burglaries in France?" she asked drily. "And if not, why not? I must go to my bank and see the manager about this; it is only in the Rue Scribe. Shall I find you here when I come back?"

"I shall be here, madame."

Pépi held open the door for her as she hurried out, closed it after her and threw himself into an armchair.

"And every single word I have said was the simple truth. Extraordinary. Unbelievable. *Formidable.*"

He relapsed into reverie.

Some time later Miss Scroby, dressed for the street in her severe gray coat and skirt and her small black hat, walked straight into the lounge. It was still occupied only by Pépi, who, naturally, sprang to his feet when she came in.

"I am sorry to have been so long," she said. "The bank manager wanted to argue."

"No doubt," said Pépi, "he considered it his duty to—"

"To try to convince me that I am a fool. I may be, but I prefer to find it out for myself. Monsieur Morand, I have the money here." She opened a substantial handbag and took out a large and bulging envelope. "I made them count it three separate times, so I assume that the amount is correct." She offered him the envelope.

"You wish me to c-count it again for you, m-madame?" stammered Pépi.

"No, of course not. I wish you, if you will be so good, to take it to the Hôtel Akela for me and pay it to the proprietor as the deposit."

Pépi took the envelope. Here it was at last, just when he was finally running out of money. Here it was, all in ordinary French currency as required; all he had to do was to say "Yes, madame, certainly," walk out of the hotel, and catch the next train from the Gare d'Austerlitz for Orléans and the South. Here it was, his "prospect" turned to a certainty, completed, achieved.

"You will, of course," went on Miss Scroby, "obtain a formal receipt for it stating clearly what the money is to pay for. A lawyer will be required to carry out the legal transfer of the property, but that will do tomorrow. Monsieur Morand, what is the matter? You do not look well."

He laid the envelope down upon the table.

"I—it is true, I do not feel well. Madame, it would be better if you took this money to the Akela yourself."

"But I understood that it would be better if I did not appear in the matter until the preliminaries are settled."

Pépi took out his handkerchief and wiped his brow.

"Madame would do better to find some other person to do her this service—some trustworthy person," he said, and broke into a nervous laugh.

Miss Scroby settled herself in her chair, folded her hands in her lap and regarded him steadily.

"I thank Madame for her confidence in me, but she had better find someone else."

Still she did not speak and the envelope lay on the table between them.

"I can't go on with it," he said desperately. "Madame, I am a confidence trickster, after your money. That is how I make my living, do you understand? Now I cannot do it, I cannot go on. You are too honest for me, too truthful, too kind." He picked up his hat. "Good-bye, madame, I am going now," and he turned towards the door.

"Monsieur Morand, a moment, please. You see, I know all about you."

"You—you—"

"I cannot understand why practically every man I meet should take me for a half-wit. Do I look it?"

"Madame—"

"Young man, you are incredibly silly. Did you really think I supposed you willing to dance attendance upon me for a paltry fee as my courier?"

"Madame, I—"

"Stop talking and listen to me. When you first attached yourself to me I wondered why, and what you were. So I went to a private enquiry agent, here in Paris, and he supplied me with an outline of your career. Probably incomplete, but revealing."

Pépi dropped his hat, sank into a chair, and clutched his head in both hands.

"I decided," continued Miss Scroby in her crisp voice, "that your original conviction was probably undeserved."

Pépi lifted a scarlet face long enough to say that on his honor, it was.

"You have not been so careful of your honor since then, have you? However, I do realize that, after that, it would be difficult for you to obtain employment at your own trade."

Pépi mumbled something about being blacklisted.

"I feel compelled to say that I think a man of stronger character would have fought his way back without relapsing into crime. However, I suppose you can't help being a rather weak character. What you need is a firm backing by someone."

"Yes, madame, that has always been true." Pépi pushed his hair back, picked up his hat, and stood up. "Permit me to thank you for all your kindness to me, which was even greater than I realized. With your permission, I will go."

"The Hôtel Akela," said Miss Scroby deliberately, "will require a manager."

"Eh?" said Pépi, staring.

"Monsieur Morand, will you take the post?"

Pépi was quite incapable of answering, but Miss Scroby did not seem to mind.

CHAPTER XVII
Stag Upon the Mountain

PÉPI and Miss Scroby spent the evening celebrating, in her case the inception of a new career as hotel proprietor and in his case something like a rebirth. They ended up, very late, eating sandwiches at the Mère Catherine at Montmartre and listening to a young man singing to a mandolin.

"How marvelous," said Pépi wonderingly, "to be able to speak the truth for the rest of my life."

"Do you really suppose you will be able to keep it up?"

"Madame, I—"

"In an hotelier, a little manipulation of the truth may occasionally be necessary. It is then called tact."

Pépi choked over his wine and apologized.

The next morning she said that she was tired. "I am not accustomed to late nights, I shall take things easy today. You had better do the same. Go out and divert yourself; we will see a lawyer about the transfers tomorrow. The deposit has been paid over, so that is settled. Here is the check for your first month's salary as manager."

He went out, walking on air. He cashed the check, since he was down to his last five thousand francs, and then bought himself something he had earnestly desired for a long time, an American Dacron shirt. The day was warm and fine, he did not need to wear a waistcoat over his beautiful shirt, he could wear his coat open and show it off. With a new bow tie he thought he looked very well. There was pride in his carriage and confidence in his step. He was hotelier again, an honorable and respected profession; his past was dead and should never rise again. He hummed a tune as he walked along the Boulevard des Capucines; he sat down at a café table on the pavement and ordered a small glass of wine with an air of authority. Presently he would decide where to lunch.

An old man shuffled along the pavement selling newspapers, and Pépi bought one to read in the intervals of sipping his wine and watching

the passersby. Presently a headline caught his eye. "Consul-General As-
saulted and Robbed," it said. "Outrage in Paris."

It appeared that the Consul-General of the small South American state
of Campos de Oro had been attacked in the dusk of the previous evening
by thugs who set upon him in a quiet alley which was a short cut to the
Camposian Consulate for one approaching it from the Rue St. Honoré.
The unfortunate gentleman had been struck a violent blow upon the head
which had rendered him completely unconscious; while in this pitiable
condition he had been robbed of his wallet, his gold watch and chain, a
gold ring which he wore upon the first finger of his left hand, and a dispatch case containing documents which were, the paper understood, of
the utmost importance.

"When documents have been stolen," mused Pépi, "they are always
of the utmost importance." He read on.

"His Excellency the Consul-General is unable to supply any detailed
description of his assailants since he was most cowardly attacked from
behind. He says that he was seized by the collar and jerked backwards, he
can remember no more. He thinks that there were two men concerned in it
and that one was larger and heavier than the other. As our readers are no
doubt aware, one of the effects of severe concussion is to wipe from the
victim's mind any recollection of the last few seconds preceding the in-
jury which caused the concussion, thus the police are deprived of any
assistance they might have obtained from His Excellency's own account
of the outrage. However, no efforts are being spared—"

Pépi laid down the paper and frowned. He was recalling a short lec-
ture once delivered by Jules on the subject of Attack From Behind. If the
intended victim, said Jules, were of the classy type with a stiff collar and
a tie, and especially if he were the skinny type with a neck like a chicken,
a strong jerk from a finger inserted in the back of the collar puts pressure
on the front of the throat. "Here, see?" said Jules, laying a thick forefinger
across his own windpipe. "Then he can't even squeak and you can get on
with the job in peace. Only takes one hand, see? Throttling takes both."

Jules and Fingers? Very possibly, but it was no business of Pépi's, let
the police get on with it. Pépi had not given a thought to his previous
accomplices for days, but this paragraph had brought them back to mind.
If Scroby had returned from Chartres he would be in danger.

Pépi threw down the paper impatiently, but the warmth had gone out
of the sunlight and the savor from the wine. Better go along to the Lune
d'Italie and ask if Scroby were there.

He looked up at the sound of an English voice and there, within a few feet of him, was Scroby in person, together with an extremely pretty dark girl with an American accent.

"No, let's not go there," she said. "We've been there twice. Let's go somewhere we've not been before."

There was a pedestrian crossing at that point; Scroby and Virginia were standing at the edge of the pavement almost within Pépi's reach, waiting for a pause in the traffic.

"Somewhere on the Left Bank?" said Scroby. "Someone told me of a frightfully good place on the Quai des Grands Augustins; now, what was it? Don't fluster me, darling. The Lapérouse, that's it. Ever been there? No, then let's whistle up a taxi."

"Let's go by Métro," said Virginia, "since Mother isn't with us for once. Poor Mother, how she does hate the Métro."

"I shall lose us," said Scroby.

"I shan't. I never lose myself by Métro. Come on, Richard, it's only just round the corner."

They changed their minds about crossing the road and walked past Pépi instead, towards the Place de l'Opéra. He looked after them doubtfully; the Left Bank was not the safest part of Paris for Richard Scroby.

Pépi sprang to his feet, threw a note down upon his table, signaled the waiter that the money was there, and dashed after Scroby and the American girl. He was a little behind them descending the steps of the Opera station, and traveled at the far end of their carriage as far as Reaumur-Sebastopol, where he heard them pointing out to each other which way to go to find the train to St. Michel. He was therefore already on the platform by the time they reached it and he traveled in quite another part of the train. When Virginia Townsend and her escort emerged into the light at the Place St. Michel, Pépi was already standing on the edge of the pavement lighting a cigarette, with his back to them and his hat over his eyes.

It will be remembered that Fingers Dupré and his solid friend Jules had most successfully raided wallets in the Place de la Bastille and subsequently lost them all, even their own. Jules left his watch at the café to pay for what they had had there and together they wandered out into the night.

"Now we have nothing," said Jules, and Fingers nodded.

"What do we do?" added Jules.

"Leave Paris," said Fingers with an unaccustomed oath, for normally he did not waste even one word.

"No money," said Jules mournfully. "Let us go and get some out of Pépi."

"Where?" said Fingers.

"We can find out," said Jules, and they made enquiries about their old friend for whom, they said, they had some good news. But Pépi, by that time, was living sedately at the Couronne de Navarre attending upon Miss Scroby, and the underworld had lost sight of him.

"We will stow away on a *camion* out of Les Halles," said Jules, referring to the lorries which come into Paris late at night loaded with vegetables and other country produce and leave again very early in the morning. But they were seen and, when it was found that they had no money, were cast forth with contumely. The fact was that, even among birds of their own feather in the underworld, these two were not liked.

When they arrived at being actually hungry, Fingers took up once more his old trade in fear and trembling that some occult power should snatch his earnings from him. He gathered in a few wallets, but they were not well lined and the partners' landlady began to dun them for the rent. Finally Fingers bungled a little operation on a man who was not so drunk as he looked and the pickpocket had to run for it.

"There is a curse on us," said Jules.

"Find something bigger," said Fingers, "and then go." So they watched and waited and found the Consul-General of Campos de Oro.

There was not a great deal of money in the wallet but enough to be very useful; the gold watch and chain were rewarding and so was the heavy signet ring of soft, almost pure, gold. This was better and they rejoiced even more when they read in the paper that the Consul-General had no idea what they looked like and that no one else had noticed them.

"Our luck has turned," said Jules happily. "We struck a bad patch, that is all. Such things happen to all men at times. What are these papers in the case? I cannot read this foreign stuff and the French bits do not seem to mean anything."

Here he was wrong, for the papers were important enough to cause a great deal of trouble and delay if they were lost. The Consul-General made a loud fuss and even the French Government was seriously annoyed.

"Curse these mutton-headed half-witted representatives of rotten little one-horse states," said the French privately among themselves. "You cannot trust them with a letter to the post. They want nursemaids specially trained in the care and protection of idiot children." In public, the French said that an outrage committed upon the person of the representative of one of France's most esteemed allies was an assault upon the honor and dignity of the whole of Metropolitan France and would be avenged with the most unheard-of vigor of the law. The Sûreté was told to get on with it.

The Sûreté made some enquiries where they would do most good and within twelve hours had uncovered a man who had bought a gold watch. He was persuaded to remember the names of the men who had sold it to him.

"Oh, those two," said the Sûreté. "Yes, of course. Let the persons of Fingers Dupré and Jules the Cosh be collected and produced at once. Notify all stations and substations, urgent."

Fingers Dupré took the dispatch case from Jules and looked through the contents.

"Spanish," he said, and shook his head. "These French pages, I do not understand. Some agreement, perhaps."

"Worth money?" asked Jules.

"Possibly."

"We will take them to Guillaume le Clerc, he'll know. He will not give us much, a little something to add to the rest, and then we will go to Marseilles. We will lunch and then go, *hein?*"

Fingers nodded. They packed up the few trifles which they had not already pawned and left the house. They were lucky, because hardly were they out of sight when the police arrived and searched their rooms with painful thoroughness.

William the Clerk, who knew about documents, lived in a street just off the Quai des Grands Augustins.

Richard Scroby and Virginia Townsend strolled hand in hand across the Place St. Michel towards the river and looked, away to their right, at the twin towers of Notre Dame

"Have you ever been up there," he asked, "all among the gargoyles?"

"Not yet, no."

"Well, shall we go?"

"After lunch," said Virginia firmly. "It looks to me as if it would be quite a walk up to the top of those towers; I guess it's steps, steps, all the way? How Mother would love it. Say we go up after lunch, shall we? I'll feel more like mountaineering with some food inside me. Where's this restaurant you talked about, the Lapérouse, is it?"

"Round to the left, then. I don't know exactly how far, but it's just along here somewhere."

So they turned left along the Quai des Grands Augustins and Pépi followed after, ten yards behind.

Jules and Fingers Dupré had called upon William the Clerk but he was not at home. He was out on business. Was there any message?

Fingers shook his head and Jules asked when Guillaume was expected to return.

"At any time now, at any moment. In any case, to have his lunch, which is now all but ready. You return, yes?"

They agreed and walked away, the Camposian documents still in Jules' inside pocket.

"We also lunch, eh?" he said. "Then we go straight for the train from Guillaume's place."

Fingers nodded; they turned a couple of corners in that maze of small streets and alleys and came out upon the Quai des Grands Augustins. There were a number of people on the not too wide pavement; outside a picture shop there was a group of young art students arguing together.

"Color in masses," said one, "is as dead as Methusaleh."

"The new freedom," agreed his friend, "is to be found in line, abstract line. The new masters are those who grasp this truth."

Fingers and Jules circled round the edge of this group and came face to face with a fair-haired Englishman walking with a girl. Recognition was immediate and mutual.

"Scroby!" gasped Fingers, and turned to run.

"The English *flic!*" said Jules, and rushed after Fingers.

It is a human instinct to run after anyone who runs away from one-self, and Scroby yielded to it.

"Wait here," he said to Virginia, "shan't be a minute—" And he tore after the fugitives.

"Here," said Virginia blankly, "what is all this—"

Someone brushed past her, a neat little man in a neat gray suit. He did not look like an athlete but he showed a surprising turn of speed; he was even gaining upon Scroby. Virginia had an acute sense of being left out of things.

"Richard!" she said indignantly, and ran like a mad thing after Pépi. Passersby on the pavement scattered, dodged with cries of alarm, divided to let the hunt go by, and stopped to stare after it. The pursuit turned into the first street it came to and one by one passed from sight.

Two American soldiers, on leave in Paris, paused in their stroll to observe these happenings.

"We-ell," said one on a long note of surprise. "What's cooking?"

"Guess it's just some kind of native custom," said the other. "C'mon."

They resumed their stroll.

The Sûreté orders to arrest Dupré and Jules were filtering rapidly through the usual channels, and Police-Constable Pignol's Sergeant had just informed him of the order. Pignol was on his beat and the Sergeant was going his rounds to alert his patrols one after another, for this district was where the two criminals lived.

"You understand," said the Sergeant, "do you? These two men are to be arrested at sight; the descriptions are as follows." He read them out. "Got that?"

"Yes, *mon Sergent.*"

"Well, keep your eyes skinned."

"Yes, *mon Sergent.*"

The Sergeant strode rapidly away; as he turned the corner of the street he looked back. Pignol, with his hands clasped lightly behind his back, was gazing intently at a display of fruit outside a greengrocer's shop. The Sergeant shook his head angrily and went on.

Constable Pignol was large, fat, and fifty, nearly due for retirement. He had served in the Paris police for almost thirty years faithfully, industriously, and quite without either distinction or promotion. He came from the South and looked forward to going back there when he retired; he came of a family of fruit growers and when he was his own master with a pension for life he would have an orchard and grow apples and pears, plums and peaches. Beautiful, plump, succulent peaches like those in the tray before him now, laid out upon cotton wool and having each a cummerbund of blue tissue paper wound round it. He gazed upon those delectable peaches and fell into a waking dream of culture and pruning, blossom and harvest.

There was something moving on the stall which had not been there a moment earlier; Pignol rubbed his eyes and looked again. It was like a monkey; it was a monkey. Someone's pet, escaped, for it wore a red jacket and a little cap to match and was plainly not afraid of him. It ran along the back of the stall, helped itself to one of the peaches, and sat back to eat it with obvious enjoyment, eyes rounded, little paws busy, and the juice running down its chin.

Pignol liked the look of the monkey, but theft could not be allowed. He took two heavy paces forwards and flapped at the creature with a large hand.

"Shoo," he said, "shoo. Go away."

The monkey threw away the peach stone, leapt at Pignol's hand, ran up his arm to his shoulder, and jumped from there to a lamppost on the pavement. Pignol revolved upon his axis and looked up. The monkey ran up the post, climbed to the top of the lantern, and there vanished.

Pignol stood transfixed, staring up, and then it was as though a whirl-wind caught him. He found himself running furiously along the street, not only running but proceeding in standing leaps. He felt as though he were borne up by some strange power, his feet hardly touched the ground; he had not moved so fast for years and years, not since he was a gangling lad robbing a neighbor's orchard and the farmer after him with a pitchfork.

His Sergeant, passing the end of the street, looked up it to see, with paralyzing stupefaction, his fat elderly Constable running and leaping like a stag upon the mountains.

"What the devil—" said the Sergeant.

The Constable made a skid-turn at the entrance to an alley between houses and disappeared from sight. The Sergeant came to himself with a jerk and set off in pursuit.

Along the twisting alley between garbage cans, through a court into another alley, round two corners, and there—

CHAPTER XVIII
All's Well

FINGERS, with Jules following hot upon his heels, ran up the side turning from the Quai des Grands Augustins. Behind them came Scroby, gradu-ally lessening the gap because Jules was not in any real sense a runner; after Scroby came Pépi, urged to superhuman efforts by the awful dread that if Scroby were killed his aunt would immediately abandon Paris and the Hôtel Akela together; last of all came Virginia, who normally could run very well but not in the "pencil-slim" skirt of the prevailing mode.

Fingers knew this part of Paris as the toddler knows the nursery floor, by close and lifelong study. He dived through an archway, across a court-yard, and down an alley leading out of it until he reached a sharp right-angled turn. He spun round this and stopped, out of sight of any pursuer, and took a cosh from his pocket as Jules turned the corner and lurched to a stop behind him to lean, panting, against the wall. Five seconds later light, flying footsteps heralded the arrival of Scroby; Fingers drew him-self together and the arm holding the cosh went back.

The moment the flaxen head came round the corner the arm came down like a flail and there was a sharp thud. Scroby staggered, his eyes closed, his knees bent under him, and he went down in an untidy heap. Fingers raised the cosh again, but before a second blow could land, Pépi swung round the corner.

"Stop it—stop it—"

Fingers laughed, for there was nothing about Pépi, Nature's noncombatant, for any man to fear. Fingers merely flicked out with the cosh and caught Pépi across the nose, which reacted in the usual manner. Pépi stepped back and became aware of blood pouring from his nose, dripping and running down the front of his beautiful, spotless white Dacron shirt, his pride, his delight, the emblem of his new life.

It has been said that for every man there is some one thing for which he will fight—

Pépi uttered a scream of rage, sprang at Fingers, and swung a most unscientific "haymaker"; Fingers, who was not even looking at him, received it right on the chin. He went back against the wall, slid down it quite slowly, and fell on his face in the gutter.

Jules managed, with an effort, to draw his first long breath since he stopped running. He advanced, vast, ponderous, and menacing; into Pépi's mind there flashed the memory of something a man had told him in prison, a little man like himself. Pépi put his head down and charged like an infuriated goat. Jules, hit squarely in the wind, staggered and tripped over Fingers.

At this crucial moment there arrived Virginia Townsend, who took one horrified glance at the battlefield and screamed for help at the pitch of extremely healthy lungs.

When Constable Pignol came up from the further side of the battle, he heard first Virginia's yells and then, between them, in a solemn ground-bass, a deep and hollow sound as of a bell tolling for an execution. He rounded the last corner in kangaroo-like hops to find two unconscious men on the ground, a girl shrieking like a ship's siren, and a small man extensively bloodstained who was furiously banging the head of yet a fourth man against an empty dustbin. Pignol had considerable difficulty in detaching the small man; by the time he had done so his Sergeant arrived, running.

"What! Who—who are— Oh! You've got them!"

Pignol straightened to attention.

"Yes, *mon Sergent.*" It was always safe to say "Yes, *mon Sergent,*" to go on with; what the Sergeant might be talking about usually became clear in the end.

Virginia sat down on the dirty ground and transferred Scroby's head from the mud to her lap. The movement revived him; he opened his eyes and sat up unsteadily. He focused his eyes with difficulty upon the pleasant sight of the Sergeant handcuffing Fingers and Jules together; they were still unconscious, but there is no sense in taking risks. Pignol, a kind man at heart, was helping Pépi to wipe himself down, though the operation was not a great success.

Virginia could bear it no longer.

"Now will someone please tell me what is all this?"

"Two criminals, madame, whom we, the police, have just arrested. May I know Madame's name?"

Virginia told him. "And this is Monsieur Richard Scroby, my fiancé."

"My felicitations, mademoiselle."

"Thank you. But, Richard, why were you chasing—"

"Two blighters I had a spot of trouble with once before. Nothing much."

"You didn't tell me—"

"Oh, I forgot," said Scroby vaguely, and got to his feet.

Virginia turned to Pépi.

"This brave man came to your rescue, did you know? I think it was the bravest thing I've ever seen! He just hurled himself at those two."

"Oh? Oh, thanks awfully."

Pépi, still a most distressing sight, managed a courtly bow. "A pleasure, mademoiselle—monsieur."

"But who are you?" asked Virginia.

Pépi drew himself up.

"Philippe Morand, at your service, mademoiselle."

"But—" said Scroby.

"I have the honor to be in the employment of your distinguished aunt, Miss Scroby."

"In her employment?"

"Yes, monsieur. I am the manager of her hotel. The Hôtel Akela, in the Rue Vignon."

"Oh, I see. She is staying there."

"Oh no, monsieur. She is staying at the Couronne de Navarre in the Chaussée d'Antin. The Hôtel Akela, that she has just purchased."

"Purchased—"

"Yes, monsieur. And I am her manager."

"You know," said Scroby to Virginia, "I thought I was quite all right but I'm not, you know. I thought I heard this chap say that my aunt had bought a hotel in the Rue Vignon."

"That's right, darling. I heard it too."

"Oh? But—"

"Excuse me, monsieur," said the Sergeant, "if I might pass by you in this inconveniently narrow passage? I wish to telephone for a police van to remove this garbage." He waved his hand over Jules and Fingers, still sleeping.

"Garbage?" said Scroby. "Oh yes, those two. Yes. Who are they, do you know?"

"But, yes, monsieur. The underneath one is Fingers Dupré, a pick-pocket; the larger one on the top is called Jules the Cosh, a robber. They are wanted for robbery with violence."

No one happened at the moment to be looking at Constable Pignol, which was rather a pity, for the slow ecstatic dawn of happy comprehension is always a delicious sight. So that was who they were, no wonder *mon Sergent* was pleased. But Pignol said nothing and the moment passed; the Sergeant went away to call up his station with the good news and Scroby, Virginia, and Pépi looked at each other.

"I think," said Scroby, "that a drink would do us all good. Monsieur—er—"

"Morand—"

"Morand, we hope for the pleasure of your company. Did you really lay out those two thugs? Stout fellow. Virginia—"

"I thank Monsieur a thousand times," said Pépi, "but I must beg to be excused—my face—my shirt. Especially my shirt! I am not a fit." He bowed deprecatingly.

"My heavens, I owe you a shirt and a whole lot more besides. A taxi to my hotel for a start and then you can tell me all about Aunt Angela's hotel. Er," addressing Pignol, "you can manage alone, I think?"

"*Mais oui, monsieur,*" said Pignol, displaying a fist like a rolled ham.

"Good luck," said Scroby, deftly tucking a couple of thousand-franc notes into the fist, "and thank you."

Pignol saluted smartly.

When the Sergeant came back he looked at Pignol with an odd expression of unwilling respect.

"Well, you've pulled off something for once," he said. "Thank you, *mon Sergent.*"

"How did you know they were here?"

"I did not know, *mon Sergent.*"

"Then what—"

Pignol hesitated. It would be of no use telling the Sergeant that he had been hurtled there by incomprehensible powers; Pignol could not understand it himself and one could not expect the Sergeant to believe it. Better say something that was true and discard the rest.

"I heard the lady scream, *mon Sergent*."

"Oh, I see. You can run when you like, can't you?"

Pignol smiled modestly; it seemed the only thing to do.

James and Charles Latimer, themselves unseen, waited until police reinforcements came and removed the persons of Fingers Dupré and Jules the Cosh to custody in a squad car, "for," said James, "these men are as vicious as mad dogs and as wily as serpents, there may yet be some slip 'twixt cup and lip."

"I am of your opinion, yes, Cousin. Let us escort them all the way till the cell doors close upon them, so we may be certain that this part of our task is indeed well done."

"And the Constable? Will his witches' gallop prey upon his mind, Charles, how say you?"

"Not a whit, Cousin. Already he does not believe it quite; he is persuading himself it could not happen, ergo, it did not. In a month's time he will only remember how fast he ran."

James laughed; the squad car drew up at the Quartier police station in the Rue de l'Abbaye, and the prisoners were conducted inside. They had recovered consciousness by this time but did not look a great deal the better for it. Doors clanged behind them and keys turned.

"That completes that," said James. "The third rogue has seen the light and will, I think, be a rogue no more. He was never, I believe, a very wholehearted criminal."

"He had leanings towards respectability," agreed Charles. "The other part of our task is also done, for I think our Richard will not now be deflected from matrimony, whatever his aunt may say. We may now go home where we belong, James, may we not? For I feel that this time we hold no place in this world which we may be sorry to leave."

James nodded but made no comment and they walked slowly through the sunlit streets to lunch once more at the Café Grecque and then to the Lune d'Italie and up to Scroby's rooms, where they found Wilkins alone.

"I am sorry, gentlemen, but Mr. Scroby is out. He and Miss Townsend and a French gentleman have gone to call, as I understand, upon Miss Scroby, who is said to be staying in a hotel called the Couronne de Navarre. I regret that I am not aware when Mr. Scroby may be expected to return."

Charles, who seemed to have recovered his spirits, beamed upon

Wilkins and asked whether Mr. Scroby and the other gentleman bore any signs of conflict. Wilkins looked gently amused.

"You knew that there had been a little excitement, sir? The damage does not appear to be serious. Mr. Morand, if I have the French gentleman's name correctly, was pleased to avail himself of my assistance, sir. I have had some experience in affairs of that sort. I procured a new shirt for Mr. Morand while he applied cold compresses to his nose, sir. When he left here he was completely presentable after the French manner."

"The French manner—"

"No doubt my tastes are insular, sir, but I cannot reconcile myself to a bow tie. Can I offer the gentlemen any little refreshment of any kind?"

They went in; as they did so hurried footsteps followed them down the passage and Scroby dashed in.

"I hoped I'd find you here! I say, everything's fine and Aunt Angela more human than I've ever known her. Virginia managed; I knew she would. They didn't seem to want me so I came away. She's telling Virginia how ill I was when I had measles. Let's have a drink—Wilkins! Aunt Angela seemed a bit apologetic about something, I don't know what. It doesn't matter. She's got her hotel and I've got Virginia and it's a lovely day and all's well. What are you having?"

When they had rejoiced with him James asked, with his usual grave courtesy, whether he and Charles might trespass upon Scroby's kindness for a small service.

"Why, of course! What is it?"

"If we might borrow your car and Wilkins as driver—"

"Of course! When, tonight?"

"Tomorrow, if we might. We have to go to St. Denis-sur-Aisne. If that is not too far—it is rather a long way."

"Not too far at all. When I think that if it hadn't been for you I shouldn't have met Virginia—"

Since Fingers Dupré and Jules the Cosh seemed to have passed without trace from Scroby's happy mind, the Latimers did not recall them.

"Tomorrow, did you say? Look," said Scroby, "I'll come with you for the run if you don't mind starting early. We could lunch there, couldn't we? The fact is, Virginia's fixing up a lunch party tomorrow for Aunt Angela to meet Mrs. Townsend and I think if I had another engagement it would fit in quite well—I mean, I think they'll get on quite well without me—I mean, I rather shrink, if you understand, do you?"

James smiled and then laughed, his odd short laugh a little like a barking dog.

"I remember when I first met my future mother-in-law," he said. "My dear wife's family were enthusiastic Tractarians, and when honesty forced me to admit that we Latimers were Evangelical to the backbone her horror was such that you might have thought we were plague-ridden."

"Very awkward," said Scroby, who had only the vaguest idea of the issue involved. "I hope she soon got over it," as though Tractarianism were something like sciatica. "Shall we start at nine tomorrow if that's not too early?"

They reached St. Denis-sur-Aisne soon after noon to be enthusiastically greeted by the proprietor of the Hôtel du Commerce. They lunched very well and the Latimers arranged to leave their luggage at the hotel as formerly.

"The messieurs will not require it for some little time?" asked the proprietor, whose wife had dinned into his head the idea that this arrangement was a little unusual.

"Oh no," said Charles cheerfully. "You see, we are going home where we shall have all that we need. These cases merely contain our traveling necessities."

"And to leave them here," said the proprietor, "saves exertion and trouble in transport, naturally. Weight, also, if one goes by air. How sensible."

"When you say 'by air,'" began James, but Charles interposed hastily.

"All experienced travelers," he said, "aim to travel light. Yes, sir, and we have solved the problem. We travel lighter than any by carrying no baggage at all. You are sure these things are of no inconvenience to you here?"

"None—none! Most happy, at all times, to serve the messieurs."

"I think," said Scroby, "I'll send Wilkins to get the car filled up before we start back; it will save having to stop on the road."

"Do, my dear Richard, do," said James. "The garage is but a hundred yards further along the road there and André the *garagiste* is a most obliging fellow."

"You know this place well, don't you?" said Scroby, when Wilkins had driven off.

"Why, yes, sir," said Charles. "You might say, in a sense, that we live here."

Scroby looked a little startled.

"Shall we take a short stroll till Wilkins returns?" said James. "A little gentle exercise after a meal is beneficial to the digestion."

They moved off along the road together and the Latimers commented upon such small changes as had occurred in St. Denis in the past year.

"Aristide Vigneron has repainted the windows of his Emporium," said Charles. "Look, James, all five windows and the doors, too."

"But not the upper windows," said James disapprovingly. "The French have no grasp of the importance of preserving woodwork."

"But the chemist has put in a new window altogether," said Charles. "Here comes Sergeant Boulestier, stout and dignified as ever."

The Sergeant passed by on the other side of the road and returned a salute to the Latimers' gestures of greeting.

"Where does this road go to?" asked Scroby, who felt that he was getting out of his depth.

"Mézières," said Charles, "and, eventually, Sedan." They reached the gate of the cemetery as he spoke; he laid his hand upon it and swung it open.

Scroby hesitated, but James said: "What is that?" and they passed in together. James was pointing at a square of neatly shaven turf with a large wreath lying upon it. A fresh wreath, for the flowers were bright and stiff. There was something sitting in the middle of it, a small monkey in a red jacket; he had taken a rose from the wreath and was pulling off the petals one by one and tossing them in the air.

"Ulysses!" called Charles in a commanding voice. "Stop that at once!"

Ulysses looked round and immediately vanished and there was silence. Scroby began to say something but broke off and looked round. He was quite alone; there was no one in sight in the cemetery or on the road outside except a young lad in a creaking farm cart drawn by an old white horse. He went past, merely glancing at Scroby as he went.

Scroby drew himself up; it took a conscious effort. He walked forward to the grave upon which the wreath lay; in the middle of the wreath he saw the long stem of a rose which had been largely denuded of its petals. Bright scraps of color lay about the grass.

At the head of the grave there was a granite cross with an inscription, deeply incised, to the memory of James and Charles Latimer, who died upon the first of September 1870.

THE END

Rue Morgue Press Titles as of August 2000

Brief Candles by Manning Coles. From Topper to Aunt Dimity, mystery readers have embraced the cozy ghost story. Four of the best were written by Manning Coles, the creator of the witty Tommy Hambledon spy novels. First published in 1954, *Brief Candles* is likely to produce more laughs than chills as a young couple vacationing in France run into two gentlemen with decidedly old-world manners. What they don't know is that James and Charles Latimer are ancestors of theirs who shuffled off this mortal coil some 80 years earlier when, emboldened by strong drink and with only a pet monkey and an aged waiter as allies, the two made a valiant, foolish and quite fatal attempt to halt a German advance during the Franco-Prussian War of 1870. Now these two ectoplasmic gentlemen and their spectral pet monkey Ulysses have been summoned from their unmarked graves because their visiting relatives are in serious trouble. But before they can solve the younger Latimers' problems, the three benevolent spirits light brief candles of insanity for a tipsy policeman, a recalcitrant banker, a convocation of English ghostbusters, and a card-playing rogue who's wanted for murder. "As felicitously foolish as a collaboration of (P.G.) Wodehouse and Thorne Smith."—Anthony Boucher. "For those who like something out of the ordinary. Lighthearted, very funny.'—*The Sunday Times*. "A gay, most readable story."—*The Daily Telegraph*. **0-915230-24-0** **$14.00**

Happy Returns by Manning Coles. The ghostly Latimers and their pet spectral monkey Ulysses return from the grave when Uncle Quentin finds himself in need of their help—it seems the old boy is being pursued by an old flame who won't take no for an answer in her quest to get him to the altar. Along the way, our courteous and honest spooks thwart a couple of bank robbers, unleash a bevy of circus animals on an unsuspecting French town, help out the odd person or two and even "solve" a murder—with the help of the victim. The laughs start practically from the first page and don't stop until Ulysses slides down the bannister, glass of wine in hand, to drink a toast to returning old friends. **0-915230-31-3** **$14.00**

The Chinese Chop by Juanita Sheridan. The postwar housing crunch finds Janice Cameron, newly arrived in New York City from Hawaii, without a place to live until she answers an ad for a roommate. It turns out the advertiser is an acquaintance from Hawaii, Lily Wu, whom critic Anthony Boucher (for whom Bouchercon, the World Mystery Convention, is named) described as "the exquisitely blended product of Eastern and Western cultures" and the only female sleuth that he "was devotedly in love with," citing "that odd mixture of respect for her professional skills and delight in her personal charms." First published in 1949, this ground-breaking book was the first of four to feature Lily and be told by her Watson, Janice, a first-time novelist. No sooner do Lily and Janice move into a rooming house in Washington Square than a corpse is found in the basement. In Lily Wu, Sheridan created one of the most believable—and memorable—female sleuths of her day. **0-915230-32-1** **$14.00**

Death on Milestone Buttress by Glyn Carr. Abercrombie ("Filthy") Lewker was looking forward to a fortnight of climbing in Wales after a grueling season touring England with his Shakespearean company. Young Hilary Bourne thought the fresh air would be a pleasant change from her dreary job at the bank, as well as a chance to renew her acquaintance with a certain young scientist. Neither one expected this bucolic outing to turn deadly but when one of their party is killed in an apparent accident during what should have been an easy climb on the Milestone Buttress, Filthy and Hilary turn detective. Nearly every member of the climbing party had reason to hate the victim but each one also had an alibi for the time of the murder. Working as a team, Filthy and Hilary retrace the route of the fatal climb before returning to their lodgings where, in the grand tradition of Nero Wolfe, Filthy confronts the suspects and points his finger at the only person who could have committed the crime. Filled with climbing details sure to appeal to both expert climbers and armchair mountaineers alike, *Death on Milestone Buttress* was published in England in 1951, the first of fifteen detective novels in which Abercrombie Lewker outwitted murderers on peaks scattered around the globe, from Wales to Switzerland to the Himalayas.

0-915230-29-1 $14.00

Black Corridors by Constance & Gwenyth Little. Some people go to the beach for their vacations, others go to the mountains. Jessie Warren's Aunt Isabel preferred checking herself intothe hospital where she thoroughly enjoyed a spot of bad health although the doctors were at a loss to spot any cause. As usual, Jessie and her sister tossed to see who would accompany Aunt Isabel to the hospital—and, as usual, Jessie lost. Jessie's mother pointed out that pampering her rich aunt might do her some good in the future, even if it means that Jessie has to miss a date or two with some promising beaux. Aunt Isabel insists on staying in her favorite room, which means the current patient has to be disposessed. And when that man's black wallet turns up missing, just about everyone joins in the hunt. That's about the time someone decided to start killing blondes. For the first time in her life Jessie's glad to have her bright red hair, even if a certain doctor—who doesn't have the money or the looks of her other beaux—enjoys making fun of those flaming locks. But after Jessie stumbles across a couple of bodies and starts snooping around, the murderer figures the time has come to switch from blondes to redheads. First published in 1940, *Black Corridors* is Constance & Gwenyth Little at their wackiest best.   **0-915230-33-X $14.00**

The Black Stocking by Constance & Gwenyth Little. Irene Hastings, who can't decide which of her two fiancés she should marry, is looking forward to a nice vacation, and everything would have been just fine had not her mousy friend Ann asked to be dropped off at an insane asylum so she could visit her sister. When the sister escapes, just about everyone, including a handsome young doctor, mistakes Irene for the runaway loony, and she is put up at an isolated private hospital under house arrest, pending final identification. Only there's not a bed to be had in the hospital. One of the staff is already sleeping in a tent on the grounds, so it's decided that Irene is to share a bedroom with young Dr. Ross Munster, much to the consternation of both parties. On the other hand, Irene's much-married mother Elise, an Auntie Mame type who rushes to her rescue, figures that the young doctor has son-in-law written all over him. She also figures there's plenty of room in that bedroom for herself as well. In the meantime, Irene runs into a headless nurse, a corpse that won't stay put, an empty coffin, a missing will, and a mysterious black stocking. As Elise would say, "Mong Dew!" First published in 1946.   **0-915230-30-5 $14.00**

The Black-Headed Pins by Constance & Gwenyth Little. "...a zany, fun-loving puzzler spun by the sisters Little—it's celluloid screwball comedy printed on paper. The charm of this book lies in the lively banter between characters and the breakneck pace of the story."—Diane Plumley, *Dastardly Deeds.* "For a strong example of their work, try (this) very funny and inventive 1938 novel of a dysfunctional family Christmas." Jon L. Breen, *Ellery Queen's Mystery Magazine.*   **0-915230-25-9 $14.00**

The Black Gloves by Constance & Gwenyth Little. "I'm relishing every madcap moment."—*Murder Most Cozy.* Welcome to the Vickers estate near East Orange, New Jersey, where the middle class is destroying the neighborhood, erecting their horrid little cottages, playing on the Vickers tennis court, and generally disrupting the comfortable life of Hammond Vickers no end. Why does there also have to be a corpse in the cellar? First published in 1939.   **0-915230-20-8 $14.00**

The Black Honeymoon by Constance & Gwenyth Little. Can you murder someone with feathers? If you don't believe feathers are lethal, then you probably haven't read a Little mystery. No, Uncle Richard wasn't tickled to death—though we can't make the same guarantee for readers—but the hyper-allergic rich man did manage to sneeze himself into the hereafter. First published in 1944. **0-915230-21-6 $14.00**

Great Black Kanba by Constance & Gwenyth Little. "If you love train mysteries as much as I do, hop on the Trans-Australia Railway in *Great Black Kanba*, a fast and funny 1944 novel by the talented (Littles)."—Jon L. Breen, *Ellery Queen's Mystery Magazine*. "I have decided to add *Kanba* to my favorite mysteries of all time list!...a zany ride I'll definitely take again and again."—Diane Plumley in the Murder Ink newsletter. When a young American woman wakes up on an Australian train with a bump on her head and no memory, she suddenly finds out that she's engaged to two different men and the chief suspect in a murder case. It all adds up to some delightful mischief—call it Cornell Woolrich on laughing gas. **0-915230-22-4 $14.00**

The Grey Mist Murders by Constance & Gwenyth Little. Who—or what—is the mysterious figure that emerges from the grey mist to strike down several passengers on the final leg of a round-the-world sea voyage? Is it the same shadowy entity that persists in leaving three matches outside Lady Marsh's cabin every morning? And why does one flimsy negligee seem to pop up at every turn? When Carla Bray first heard things go bump in the night, she hardly expected to find a corpse in the adjoining cabin. Nor did she expect to find herself the chief suspect in the murders. This 1938 effort was the Littles' first book. **0-915230-26-7 $14.00**

Murder is a Collector's Item by Elizabeth Dean. "(It) froths over with the same effervescent humor as the best Hepburn-Grant films."—Sujata Massey. "Completely enjoyable."—*New York Times*. "Fast and funny."—*The New Yorker*. Twenty-six-year-old Emma Marsh isn't much at spelling or geography and perhaps she butchers the odd literary quotation or two, but she's a keen judge of character and more than able to hold her own when it comes to selling antiques or solving murders. Originally published in 1939, *Murder is a Collector's Item* was the first of three books featuring Emma. Smoothly written and sparkling with dry, sophisticated humor, this milestone combines an intriguing puzzle with an entertaining portrait of a self-possessed young woman on her own at the end of the Great Depression. **0-915230-19-4 $14.00**

Murder is a Serious Business by Elizabeth Dean. It's 1940 and the Thirsty Thirties are over but you couldn't tell it by the gang at J. Graham Antiques, where clerk Emma Marsh, her would-be criminologist boyfriend Hank, and boss Jeff Graham trade barbs in between shots of scotch when they aren't bothered by the rare customer. Trouble starts when Emma and crew head for a weekend at Amos Currier's country estate to inventory the man's antiques collection. It isn't long before the bodies start falling and once again Emma is forced to turn sleuth in order to prove that her boss isn't a killer. "Judging from (this book) it's too bad she didn't write a few more."—Mary Ann Steel, *I Love a Mystery*. **0-915230-28-3 $14.95**

Murder, Chop Chop by James Norman. "The book has the butter-wouldn't-melt-in-his-mouth cool of Rick in *Casablanca*."—*The Rocky Mountain News*. "Amuses the reader no end."—*Mystery News*. "This long out-of-print masterpiece is intricately plotted, full of eccentric characters and very humorous indeed. Highly recommended."—*Mysteries by Mail*. Meet Gimiendo Hernandez Quinto, a gigantic Mexican who once rode with Pancho Villa and who now trains *guerrilleros* for the Nationalist Chinese government when he isn't solving murders. At his side is a beautiful Eurasian known as Mountain of Virtue, a woman as dangerous to men as she is irresistible. Together they look into the murder of Abe Harrow, an ambulance driver who appears to have died at three different times. There's also a cipher or two to crack, a train with a mind of its own, and Chiang Kai-shek's false teeth, which have gone mysteriously missing. First published in 1942. **0-915230-16-X $13.00**

Death at The Dog by Joanna Cannan. "Worthy of being discussed in the same breath with an Agatha Christie or Josephine Tey...anyone who enjoys Golden Age mysteries will surely enjoy this one."—Sally Fellows, *Mystery News*. "Skilled writing and brilliant characterization."—*Times of London*. "An excellent English rural tale."—Jacques Barzun & Wendell Hertig Taylor in *A Catalogue of Crime*. Set in late 1939 during the first anxious months of World War II, *Death at The Dog*, which was first published in 1941, is a wonderful example of the classic English detective novel that first flourished between the two World Wars. Set in a picturesque village filled with thatched-roof-cottages, eccentric villagers and genial pubs, it's as well-plotted as a Christie, with clues abundantly and fairly planted, and as deftly written as the best of the books by either Sayers or Marsh, filled with quotable lines and perceptive observations on the human condition. **0-915230-23-2 $14.00**

They Rang Up the Police by Joanna Cannan. "Just delightful."—*Sleuth of Baker Street* Pick-of-the-Month. "A brilliantly plotted mystery...splendid character study...don't miss this one, folks. It's a keeper."—Sally Fellows, *Mystery News*. When Delia Cathcart and Major Willoughby disappear from their quiet English village one Saturday morning in July 1937, it looks like a simple case of a frustrated spinster running off for a bit of fun with a straying husband. But as the hours turn into days, Inspector Guy Northeast begins to suspect that she may have been the victim of foul play. Never published in the United States, *They Rang Up the Police* appeared in England in 1939. **0-915230-27-5 $14.00**

Cook Up a Crime by Charlotte Murray Russell. "Perhaps the mother of today's 'cozy' mystery . . . amateur sleuth Jane has a personality guaranteed to entertain the most demanding reader."—Andy Plonka, *The Mystery Reader*. "Some wonderful old time recipes...highly recommended."—*Mysteries by Mail*. Meet Jane Amanda Edwards, a self-styled "full-fashioned" spinster who complains she hasn't looked at herself in a full-length mirror since Helen Hokinson started drawing for *The New Yorker*. But you can always count on Jane to look into other people's affairs, especially when there's a juicy murder case to investigate. In this 1951 title Jane goes searching for recipes (included between chapters) for a cookbook project and finds a body instead. And once again her lily-of-the-field brother Arthur goes looking for love, finds strong drink, and is eventually discovered clutching the murder weapon. **0-915230-18-6 $13.00**

The Man from Tibet by Clyde B. Clason. Locked inside the Tibetan Room of his Chicago luxury apartment, the rich antiquarian was overheard repeating a forbidden occult chant under the watchful eyes of Buddhist gods. When the doors were opened it appeared that he had succumbed to a heart attack. But the elderly Roman historian and sometime amateur sleuth Theocritus Lucius Westborough is convinced that Adam Merriweather's death was anything but natural and that the weapon was an eighth century Tibetan manuscript. If it's murder, who could have done it, and how? Suspects abound. There's Tsongpun Bonbo, the gentle Tibetan lama from whom the manuscript was originally stolen; Chang, Merriweather's scholarly Tibetan secretary who had fled a Himalayan monastery; Merriweather's son Vincent, who disliked his father and stood to inherit a fortune; Dr. Jed Merriweather, the dead man's brother, who came to Chicago to beg for funds to continue his archaeological digs in Asia; Dr. Walters, the dead man's physician, who guarded a secret; and Janice Shelton, his young ward, who found herself being pushed by Merriweather into marrying his son. How the murder was accomplished has earned praise from such impossible crime connoisseurs as Robert C.S. Adey, who cited Clason's "highly original and practical locked-room murder method." **0-915230-17-8 $14.00**

The Mirror by Marlys Millhiser. "Completely enjoyable."—*Library Journal*. "A great deal of fun."—*Publishers Weekly*. How could you not be intrigued, as one reviewer pointed out, by a novel in which "you find the main character marrying her own grandfather and giving birth to her own mother?" Such is the situation in Marlys Millhiser's classic novel (a Mystery Guild selection originally published by Putnam in 1978) of two women who end up living each other's lives after they look into an antique Chinese mirror. Twenty-year-old Shay Garrett is not aware that she's pregnant and is having second thoughts about marrying Marek Weir when she's suddenly transported back 78 years in time into the body of Brandy McCabe, her own grandmother, who is unwillingly about to be married off to miner Corbin Strock. Shay's in shock but she still recognizes that the picture of her grandfather that hangs in the family home doesn't resemble her husband-to-be. But marry Corbin she does and off she goes to the high mining town of Nederland, where this thoroughly modern young woman has to learn to cope with such things as wood cooking stoves and—to her—old-fashioned attitudes about sex. In the meantime, Brandy McCabe is finding it even harder to cope with life in the Boulder, Co., of 1978. **0-915230-15-1** **$14.95**

About The Rue Morgue Press

The Rue Morgue Press vintage mystery line is designed to bring back into print those books that were favorites of readers between the turn of the century and the 1960s. The editors welcome suggestions for reprints. To receive our catalog or make suggestions, write The Rue Morgue Press, P.O. Box 4119, Boulder, Colorado 80306. (1-800-699-6214).